The Body in the Annex

A SUNSET LODGE MYSTERY

DIANA XARISSA

❀ Created with Vellum

Chapter One

Abigail Clark frowned at the "Do Not Disturb" sign on the door.

"Sorry, but I'm going to disturb," she muttered as she raised her hand and knocked loudly. The sound seemed to echo around her. After counting to ten, she knocked again. As she knocked a third time, she picked up her master key from the cart next to her.

"Hello? Housekeeping," she said loudly as she unlocked the door and pushed it open a few inches. "Hello? Is anyone here?"

The security chain wasn't in place, which allowed her to open the door further.

"Hello? It's housekeeping. It's two o'clock. Check-out time was noon," she said as she reached for the light switch next to the door.

What she saw when the lights came on sent her back outside. She slammed the door shut and then closed her eyes and tried to think. Abigail's hands were shaking as she reached into her pocket and pulled out her cell phone.

"What's your emergency?" the voice on the other end of the phone said a moment later.

"There's a body," Abigail replied.

"A body? Take a deep breath and then start by telling me who you are and where you are," she was told.

Abigail inhaled slowly and then sighed. "I'm Abigail Clark, and I'm at Sunset Lodge. I'm cleaning the rooms, but when I opened the door to 2A, I found a body."

"I'll send an ambulance and the police," the 911 operator told her. "Are you certain the person you found is dead?"

"Yes. No. I mean, I don't know. There was a lot of blood. I can't see how he can still be alive, but I didn't check or anything. As soon as I turned on the lights, I saw him, and then I walked out of the room."

"I know Sunset Lodge has a number of buildings. Exactly where should I instruct the first responders to go?"

"The annex. It's behind the main lodge building. He – the man in the room – he requested a room out here. He said he didn't want to stay in the main building." Abigail swallowed hard. "He just arrived yesterday."

"Save everything you know about the man for the police. If he truly is dead, they'll have lots of questions."

"I don't think I'll be able to answer many of them. I barely spoke to him."

"You haven't owned Sunset Lodge for long, have you?" the other woman asked.

"We closed on the property in August, but I've only been here for two weeks. The dead man was one of my first guests," Abigail replied with a shudder. "I thought I was prepared for anything, but I never imagined something like this happening. Oh, I hear sirens."

"That will be the ambulance. It should be there momentarily. Trooper Trushell is right behind them."

Abigail walked toward the road, watching for the ambulance. It appeared a moment later. She waved to the driver as he pulled up in front of the main lodge building. It took him a moment to drive the short distance from the main lodge to the annex behind it.

"You can hang up on 911 now," the ambulance driver said as he climbed out of the vehicle.

"Oh, right," Abigail replied. "Thank you," she said into her phone before she pushed the button to end the call.

"Where's the injured man?" the second member of the ambulance crew asked as she walked toward Abigail.

"In room 2A, but I'm pretty certain he's dead."

"Show us," was the reply.

Abigail walked back past her cart full of cleaning supplies to the door, leading the other two. After taking a deep breath, she unlocked the door and pushed it open. The ambulance crew members both stepped forward and then stopped in the doorway.

"I don't think we should go in there," the man said. "That's a crime scene."

"Yeah, there isn't anything we can do for him," the woman agreed.

They both turned around and took a few steps away from the door.

"Should I shut the door?" Abigail asked.

The man shrugged. "I'm pretty sure the police will be here soon."

The words were barely out of his mouth when a state police vehicle pulled up outside the lodge. The ambulance driver waved, and the vehicle slowly drove the short distance to the annex.

"Good afternoon," the man in uniform said as he climbed out of his car. "I understand we have an injured man here."

"He's beyond help," the ambulance driver replied. "We

stopped in the doorway so we wouldn't contaminate the crime scene."

The trooper raised an eyebrow. "You're that sure he's dead?"

The two from the ambulance crew exchanged glances, and then they both nodded.

"I'd guess he bled out hours ago," the woman replied after a moment.

The trooper frowned and then looked at Abigail. "You found the, um, victim?"

She nodded nervously. "I wanted to clean his room. He was supposed to check out at noon. I assumed that he'd gone and simply left his keys in the room, so I let myself in and, well, found him."

"Save the whole story for the detective who will be here shortly," the trooper told her. "He or she will be in charge of the investigation. For now, I just need to see what's been found and then secure the scene."

Abigail gestured toward the still open door. "He's in there. The door locks automatically when you shut it. I can get you a key to the door, but I'll need to go into the main building to get it."

"How did you get in?" the man asked as he walked toward the open door.

"I have a master key for all of the doors in the annex."

He nodded and then looked into the room. After a moment, he sighed and then reached into his pocket for a pair of gloves. After pulling them on, he slowly shut the door and then turned around and looked at Abigail. "You need to stay here for now, but we're going to need a key for that room."

"Yes, of course. I'll get..." she trailed off as another car pulled up in front of the lodge.

"That will be the detective," the trooper said. He walked briskly toward the main building.

Abigail looked at the ambulance crew. They were standing at attention, watching the car that was now slowly moving toward them. Abigail's first thought as the man climbed out of the car was that he looked like someone's grandfather.

He was somewhere around six feet tall with short gray hair and a slightly rounded tummy. He was wearing a wrinkled button-down shirt and black pants with a small stain on one knee. As he shut his car door, he scanned his surroundings.

"Good afternoon," he said to Abigail when their eyes met.

"Good afternoon," she repeated automatically. He looked to be in his mid-fifties, and he looked tired. Abigail assumed he'd seen too many of the bad things in the world.

"I'm Detective Fred Williams," he added.

"Abigail Clark," she said.

"Trooper Trushell? Show me what we have," the detective snapped as he turned away from Abigail.

"She needs to unlock the door," the trooper replied.

"I'm sure she can let you use her key," the detective replied.

Abigail handed her keys to the trooper, who unlocked the door. The detective looked into the room and sighed as he pulled out his phone.

"I need a full crime scene team here immediately," he said into it a moment later. "This is a murder investigation."

Half an hour later, Trooper Trushell escorted Abigail into the main lodge building. She went behind the registration desk and unlocked the safe behind it.

"You have spare keys for every room?" the trooper asked as Abigail found the box of keys for the rooms in the annex.

"We have three keys for each room, and we never give guests more than two," she replied. "Or rather, that's the policy that the former owners used and recommended to us. As I said earlier, we haven't had many guests yet."

"We?" the man replied.

Abigail shrugged. "My sister and I are co-owners of the property."

"And where is your sister right now?"

"She still lives in New York City. We were both planning to move here, but then she was offered her dream job, and she decided to stay in the city." Abigail worked to keep her tone as neutral as possible.

"How unfortunate for you," the trooper replied.

"It's fine," Abigail replied, mostly truthfully. She used another key to open the box that held the keys for the annex rooms and then started looking through it. "Here we are," she said after a moment. "A key for 2A."

"Do you have another one?"

"I should. I only gave Mr. Morris one key, and we're supposed to have three." Abigail searched through the box, checking the large tags on each key as she went. "Yes, here's the third key," she said, holding it up.

"I hope you won't mind if I take both of them," the trooper told her.

Abigail hesitated and then shrugged. "I'm going to want to change the locks on that room after you're done with it anyway. Actually, maybe I'll just lock the door and never use that room again." She shuddered and then slammed the lid of the box down hard.

"Are you okay?"

"No, not even a little bit," she replied as tears began to stream down her cheeks. "Someone murdered one of my guests, just a few doors away from where I was sleeping. I am most definitely not okay."

"Ah, there you are," a voice said before the trooper could reply. "The crime scene team is hard at work, and I'm simply in the way out there. I have quite a few questions for you," Detective Williams told Abigail.

She nodded, wiping away her tears with the back of her hand. "I'll tell you everything I can, but it isn't much."

The detective and the trooper had a short conversation before the trooper took the spare keys and left the building.

"We have a lot to discuss. I'd prefer to do so somewhere where we'll both be comfortable," the detective said to Abigail as the door swung shut behind the trooper.

"We can sit in the guest lounge," Abigail offered, gesturing toward the other side of the room.

The space had a large brick fireplace along one wall. Comfortable couches and chairs were arranged in a half circle in front of it. Abigail hesitated before sitting on one end of one of the couches. After a moment, the detective sat down next to her. He pulled out a notebook and pen and then put his cell phone on the coffee table in front of them.

"With your permission, I'm going to record this conversation," he said, nodding toward his phone.

"Yes, of course, whatever you want to do," she replied.

"Thank you. I'm going to take notes as well, but I can't write as quickly as people tend to talk, and I sometimes miss things in my notes. It's helpful to be able to go back and listen to the conversation again at a later date."

Abigail nodded and then sat back in her seat. The detective picked up his phone and tapped the screen a few times.

"I'm recording now."

"Are you going to read me my rights?"

"I wasn't going to, as you haven't been arrested, but you do have the right to have an attorney present with you while we talk, if that was your concern."

"I don't need an attorney. I've just never been questioned by the police before. I have no idea what to expect."

"Try to think of it as a friendly conversation," he suggested. "I need you to tell me all about the man in room

7

2A, but let's start with a few basics first. As I said when I arrived, I'm Detective Fred Williams. You can call me Fred."

"I'm Abigail Clark. Obviously, call me Abigail."

He made a note. "And you're the owner of Sunset Lodge?" He made the statement a question.

She nodded. "My sister and I bought it recently. I only moved in two weeks ago."

"Why don't you tell me how you came to buy the lodge," he suggested.

Abigail took a deep breath. "That's something of a long story."

"We have time."

"I'll try to give you the condensed version, but I'll warn you that I do tend to babble when I'm nervous or upset. So please tell me if I wander too far off topic.

"My sister and I were both living in New York City, and we wanted to do something different. She found the listing for Sunset Lodge on some website, so we came and took a look around and then put in an offer, almost on impulse. That was three months ago. We closed on the property in August, and I've been here for about two weeks."

"What did you do in New York City?"

"I was the manager of a small boutique hotel in the city."

"And your sister?"

"Mandy works in theater."

"Mandy?" The man looked up from his notebook.

"She's Amanda, really, but I call her Mandy."

"And she's an actor?"

Abigail laughed. "Not at all. She studied technical theater in college. She does set design and costuming and lights and sound."

"Interesting. You said earlier that you wanted a change. Buying a lodge in the Finger Lakes seems like a big change."

It wasn't a question, but Abigail still felt as if she needed to reply. "It is a big change. I studied hotel and restaurant management in college and then moved to New York City and worked my way up from waiting tables to managing both a hotel and its restaurant. I was working crazy hours with a forty-minute commute to my apartment, and then a foreign conglomerate bought the hotel and started demanding that I cut costs in every possible way. I started job hunting, of course, but then Mandy came up with the crazy idea of buying our own hotel or restaurant or something."

"So it was all Mandy's idea?"

"When we were kids, we used to talk about owning our own business together one day. We used to talk about having a restaurant that I could manage. It was going to be a themed restaurant with Mandy designing and creating the interior and exterior based on the theme and then coming up with all sorts of creative dishes based around the theme."

"And she was going to do the cooking?"

"Mandy doesn't cook," Abigail laughed again. "I'm not sure what she was planning to do once our imaginary restaurant opened. It was all just talk, really."

"And yet here you are," Fred said.

Abigail nodded. "So, like I said, my hotel had new owners, and I was starting to dread going to work for the first time in my life. Meanwhile, Mandy had just finished working on a show that was so far off Broadway that it was barely even in New York. She was tired of struggling to find jobs and then having to work insane hours for a few crazy weeks or months before finding herself out of work again. We both just needed a change."

Fred looked around the room. "Sunset Lodge is quite a large impulse purchase."

"We're mortgaged to the hilt," Abigail admitted. "I had been saving up to buy a house, so I had enough for a down payment. It helped that the property had been on the market for eighteen months."

"So you and your sister moved here about two weeks ago?"

"I moved here about two weeks ago. Just before we were due to leave New York, while we were still wrapping up our lives there, Mandy was offered an amazing job working for an off-Broadway theater. It was too good of an opportunity for her to pass up, so she stayed behind in the city."

"So she's leaving you to do all of the work of running the lodge on your own?"

"It's fine. It's mostly fine, anyway. As I said, it was too good of an opportunity for her to pass up. If she impresses the right people with this job, she could be working on Broadway in another six months. That's been her dream since we were children."

"But it does leave you with a lot more work," Fred suggested.

"Yes, but it also means that one of us has a steady income. Mandy will be making enough from her new job to help pay for everything we want to do here. We did have to change some of our plans," Abigail admitted. "Mandy was planning to redecorate the entire place, starting with the cottages. Each one was going to get its own theme based on a classic novel."

"How many cottages are there?"

"Four. There are ten rooms here in the main building and six additional rooms in the annex. I'm staying in one of the annex rooms at the moment while I work out exactly what I want to do in here and with the cottages."

"You aren't going to be giving them themes then?"

"That's still going to happen someday, but for now I think I'm just going to replace the flooring and paint all of them."

"I know Jack and Janet struggled with the upkeep in the last few years."

Abigail nodded. "They did their best, but they were ready to be done with the place eighteen months ago."

"Jack is close to seventy, I believe, and Janet isn't much younger."

"We talked to them for hours when we came to see the property. They told us all about how it had been in the family for decades and how they'd hoped that their own children would one day take over. But their daughter is a doctor in Virginia, and their son is a university professor in California. Neither of them was interested in coming back to New York or in changing careers, and apparently the grandchildren weren't interested either."

"I can't say that I blame them. Nightshade is a small town on a small lake in the middle of nowhere," Fred said. "Everyone in town is curious about the people who bought Sunset Lodge."

"Everyone in town is more than welcome to come out and meet me. I'm hoping to use lots of local labor for everything I want to do here, although I'll probably try to do as much of it myself as I possibly can to save money. And I'm hoping to be a part of the community once I've had a chance to find my feet a bit more."

"You've taken on quite a lot out here."

"I have, but I love a challenge. Jack and Janet told me that twenty years ago they were always fully booked during the summer months, and they made enough from June to August to pay their bills for the rest of the year. If I can rebuild the business to that point, I'll be happy. Jack and Janet never advertised and didn't even have a website for the lodge, so that's something else that's on my list of things to do. Quite near the top, really."

"But you'll want to spruce things up before you start taking pictures for the website," Fred suggested as he glanced around the room again.

Abigail swallowed a sigh as she tried to shift her weight on the slightly lumpy couch. The main lodge was a beautiful old building, but it was tired, and it would need a lot of love to get it back to its former glory. It also needed a lot of paint, flooring, cleaning, polishing, and some new furniture.

"It's a work in progress right now, even if most of the progress has only been making plans," she replied.

"It seems as if you could really use your sister's help."

"Not at all. I can run the lodge quite happily on my own," Abigail said firmly.

"Happily?"

Abigail sighed. "I was pretty happy until this afternoon."

Chapter Two

"Before we talk about today, let's talk a bit more about the lodge," Fred said. "Have you kept any of the former employees on the payroll?"

"I've kept everyone," Abigail replied. "Jack and Janet paid their wages through the end of the year, so they'll all be here until the first of January at least. I'm confident that we'll have enough guests between now and then that we'll be able to keep everyone after that. I'm counting on all of them to help me get the business up and running. They've all been here for years, of course."

"I'm fairly certain I know everyone who works here, but I want you to tell me about everyone as if I knew nothing, please."

"Marcia Burton is our cook. She makes the amazing breakfasts and dinners that are included with every stay at the lodge. She's been cooking here for over twenty years, and everything she's made since I've been here has been delicious."

"Breakfast and dinner are included in a stay?"

Abigail nodded. "That was how Jack and Janet did it, anyway. I don't plan to change that in the short term, because

I believe most of our guests will expect it. Everyone who has a room booked at the moment made their reservation with Jack or Janet. I don't know that any of them even know that the lodge has changed hands."

"But you don't have a proper restaurant, do you?"

"No, just a small dining room for our guests. At breakfast time, they can get eggs prepared however they like, but there's only one meat choice each day and Marcia rotates them, so bacon one day, then sausages, then turkey bacon, or whatever. She also does some sort of potatoes, or sometimes she'll make pancakes. We have yogurt and fruit and cereal, too."

"And dinner?" Fred asked, looking up from his notes.

Why is he writing all of this down? Abigail wondered. "We have a set menu for the week, so Monday is always baked ham with scalloped potatoes and Tuesday is always roast chicken with rice, and so on. There is always a vegetarian option, as well, and I'm hoping to introduce vegan options to attract more guests."

"What else can you tell me about Marcia?"

"She lives in a cottage on the edge of the property with her husband Howard. They have two children, but they're both adults who live elsewhere."

"Do you know where?"

Abigail frowned. "I'm pretty sure Marcia said that they are both in Florida."

Fred made another note. "Do you own Marcia's cottage, then?"

"I do."

"And she pays you rent?"

"No, the cottage is part of her compensation for the work she does here. I'm going to have my accountant take a look at how everything is structured for her and for the other staff to make sure that everything is being done correctly and that everyone is being fairly compensated."

"And so that you don't upset the taxman," Fred suggested.

"Especially that."

Fred nodded. "Do you know what Howard does for a living?"

"He works at the local zoo. Marcia said that he's the assistant manager, but that mostly means he gets to clean up after the people and not the animals. While they have specialists who take care of the animals, apparently the people are far more work."

"That doesn't surprise me. I haven't been to the zoo in years. It used to be quite small and rather, um, empty, but I've been told it's grown and improved a lot."

"I haven't been yet, but Howard did give me some free admission coupons. I'm going to have to make the effort and go soon."

Fred turned the page in his notebook. "Who else works for you here, then?"

"Our handyman is Carl Young. He's been here over thirty years, and he's responsible for most of the little jobs that need doing every day."

"I know Carl," Fred replied. "Jack's father hired him when he left high school and taught him how to do a little bit of everything."

"He told me that he's not allowed to do anything electrical apart from changing light bulbs."

"It was only a small fire," Fred said with a laugh. "I don't know that you'll ever get Carl to tell you the story, but it was an honest mistake, and no one ever blamed him for what happened."

Abigail raised an eyebrow. "I may have to get him to tell me the story one day. So far, Carl has been really helpful with a few small plumbing issues and with replacing a few broken towel racks and that sort of thing. It would be really useful if he could do some minor electrical work too, though. I want to replace just about every light fixture in the entire lodge."

"What is the lighting like outside the annex?"

"Terrible," Abigail sighed. "As I said, I'm staying out there at the moment, and I'm grateful that I'm usually in my room before sunset. There are two outdoor lights, one on each end of the building, but neither seems to do much, really."

Fred made a note. "But you were telling me about the staff. Does Carl live at the lodge?"

"He has a cottage near Marcia's. There are three cottages together in a cluster near the edge of the property. Arnold and his wife live in the third one."

"Arnold?"

"Arnold Nagel, he's our night manager."

"Before we talk about Arnold, what else do you know about Carl?"

Abigail frowned. "Not much. He's in his fifties, and he lives alone. His cottage is the smallest of the three, with only a single bedroom and a small living space. I went around all three cottages when we first toured the property, and I was surprised at how small Carl's cottage is. It's almost as small as the apartment I had in New York."

"Did you mention that to Carl?"

Abigail nodded. "He told me that he's perfectly happy with his cottage. He said more space would just mean more to clean."

Fred grinned. "He's right about that. My wife and I have more space than we need, and the house seems to need vacuuming or dusting nearly every day."

"Try being responsible for cleaning ten guest rooms, six annex rooms, and four cottages," Abigail said dryly. "I'm hoping we'll be successful enough to hire someone to help with the cleaning soon, but thus far we've only had two guests and one of them got himself murdered."

"We'll get to that in a moment," Fred said somberly. "What else can you tell me about Carl?"

Abigail thought for a moment. "I don't think I know anything else about Carl. He keeps to himself, although he does come into the main building for breakfast and dinner every day. Marcia cooks for the staff, even when we don't have any guests."

"That must get expensive for you."

"It's all tied up in the compensation that we provide to the staff. If they weren't getting fed, I'd have to pay them more money. At least this way, I get a nice meal twice a day, too."

"What does Carl do all day when you don't have guests?"

"I made a long list of jobs for him when I first arrived. He's been working his way through it since then. As I said earlier, he's been replacing towel racks and doing quite a bit of plumbing. There were several leaky pipes around the place when I got here. Once Carl has finished the list, he's going to start working on the painting and redecorating for me."

Fred made another note and then looked up. "Now tell me about Arnold."

"He's in his mid-forties, and he used to be a professional bodybuilder. He still works part-time at the local gym, working with people who want to build up their muscles. Besides that, he works here as our night manager."

"And what does that job entail?"

"He's responsible for dealing with guests from eight in the evening until eight in the morning, six nights a week."

"That's a lot of working hours."

"He isn't actually at the desk for all of those hours," Abigail explained quickly. "He's at the desk until ten, and then he's on call until six in the morning. Then he covers the desk again until eight, when I arrive. That's only when we have guests, of course. When the lodge is empty, Arnold doesn't have to come in at all."

"But you had a guest last night, so Arnold was working?"

Abigail frowned. "Actually, he was off last night. I stayed at the desk until ten and then forwarded the phones to my cell instead of Arnold's."

"Was last night his usual night off?"

"Yes, he always takes Monday nights off. He told me that Jack and Janet preferred that because the weekends usually brought the loudest and most difficult guests. By the time Mondays came around, Arnold needed a night off."

"You said you've had two guests since you arrived. When was your other guest here?"

"Jefferson Packer stayed for two nights last week. I put him in one of the rooms in here. The blue room."

"Why was he in Nightshade?"

"He works for the state as an environmental analyst. He was here to take samples of the water in the lake and of the soil in the area."

Fred nodded. "Now that you say that, I remember meeting him. He spent half an hour talking about some sort of bacteria in the lake that he found both fascinating and worrying."

Abigail laughed. "I made the mistake of joining him for dinner one night and hearing all about that same bacteria. He told me that it isn't believed to be dangerous to humans, but that it still shouldn't be here."

"But that was last week. When did your other guest arrive?"

"Yesterday."

"So Arnold had several days off between guests."

Abigail shrugged. "Even when we don't have guests, he still sits behind the desk for a few hours each night and each morning, and the hotel's phones get transferred to his cell number overnight. Guests or not, he's still working every day except Mondays."

"What else can you tell me about Arnold?"

"He's married to Karen, who is incredibly nice. She works for the local bank. I've only spoken to her a few times, because she's been spending most of her spare time with her mother, who isn't well."

Fred nodded. "I know the family. And they live in another of the staff cottages?"

"Yes, they live in the cottage that's between Marcia's cottage and Carl's. When we had a guest here, though, Arnold slept in one of the rooms in the annex so that he'd be nearby if the guest needed anything."

"I don't suppose he slept in the annex last night?"

"I don't believe so, but he has his own key to 6A, and he comes and goes as he pleases."

"Interesting. Which room is yours?"

"I've been staying in 4A."

"Why?"

Abigail frowned. "All of the annex rooms need a lot of work, but 4A isn't as bad as some of the others. When Arnold told me that he used to stay in an annex room when there were guests, I gave him his choice of rooms, and he picked 6A."

"And you put yesterday's guest in 2A," Fred said. "Do you have anything else to add to what you've told me about Arnold before you tell me about yesterday's guest?"

Abigail thought for a moment and then shrugged. "I can't think of anything else. I haven't had much of a chance to get to know him, really. I usually get my dinner after eight, once Arnold takes my place at the desk. He always eats before he comes to work. The situation is reversed at breakfast. I eat before I take his place, and then he gets something to eat on his way back to his cottage."

"And once you come to work, you stay behind the desk all day?"

"Not at all. I typically don't sit there for more than an

hour or two at a time. I have a sign that I put on the door for anyone who arrives, and I forward the landline to my cell and carry the hotel's cell phone with me while I do other things, but I have far too much to do to sit behind the desk all day."

Fred wrote something in his notebook and then sighed. "And now I need you to tell me everything about the man who arrived yesterday."

Abigail breathed in deeply as she raised her shoulders, then let the breath out as she lowered them and sat back in her seat. "He arrived just after one."

"Did he have a reservation?"

"He did not. When he arrived, I was behind the desk eating a sandwich and working through one of the boxes of paperwork that Jack and Janet left behind."

"Take me through everything that happened."

Sitting back and closing her eyes, Abigail inhaled slowly and then sighed. "I've been trying not to think about him. I can't quite believe – that is – he was so alive yesterday."

"Start at the beginning. You were sorting through paperwork?"

"Yes," Abigail nodded. "There are more boxes of old paperwork in the office than I can count, so I've been trying to go through at least one box every day. I usually go and sit behind the reception desk after lunch for an hour or two, sorting through paperwork and fighting with the computer."

"Fighting with the computer?"

"It's six or seven years old, and I don't think any of the software has been updated since it was new. I'm trying to get our website up to date, but it takes forever to upload anything. I'm going to have to break down and buy a new computer soon, but I'd prefer to wait until next year if I can, to spread out our expenses a little bit."

"So you're sorting papers and the door opens, and a man

walks into the lodge. What happened next?" Fred prompted her.

"I looked up and then stood up and asked if I could help him. He said he needed a room for the night. I told him that we aren't actually open for guests and he was very nice about it, but then he asked me where else he could stay in the area. He said he'd come to Nightshade for an important meeting and that he didn't want to have to drive miles away just to turn around and come back for his meeting," Abigail said in a rush.

"Did he say when or where this meeting was taking place?"

Abigail slowly shook her head. "I got the impression that it was happening later in the day, but he didn't actually say. He just asked if I knew of any other hotels or motels or anywhere that he could get a room for just one night. I couldn't think of anywhere and, well, I suppose I simply let him talk me into letting him stay even though we aren't supposed to be open."

"He talked you into it?"

"I'm explaining it all badly. He didn't talk me into it. He simply asked if I knew of any other options, and I didn't. He was very polite and rather charming, and I started to feel guilty about sending him away. I'd already had a guest here in spite of not being open, so I couldn't really see the harm in letting him stay as well."

"So you told him he could stay."

"I did, and he was hugely grateful. I offered him a room here, in the main building, but he actually asked if he could have a room in the annex. He said he'd stayed out there before. When he requested the annex, I wondered if he was asking because those rooms are typically less expensive, but I told him he could stay in any room he wanted for the same price, and he still chose the annex."

"Interesting," Fred said, making a note.

"Is it? I thought it was a bit odd, but it made things easier for me."

"I assume he introduced himself?"

"Oh, yes, of course. I asked for identification as well. He showed me his passport. His name was Russell Morris. He told me to call him Rusty."

Fred nodded. "What else did he have to say while he was checking in?"

"We just chatted a bit about the area. He told me that he'd been here before, both to Nightshade and to the Sunset Lodge. I asked if he still had friends here in town, and he shrugged and said something about having friends and enemies alike." Abigail felt herself flushing. "I should have asked him for more information about his enemies, shouldn't I?"

Fred shook his head. "I'm sure his remark didn't seem at all significant at the time."

"It didn't. It was just polite conversation. I ran his credit card through the machine, which took ages, and then gave him the keys to his room. He asked if meals were still included in the room rate, and I assured him that Marcia is still cooking every day." She blushed again. "He said something about maybe seeing me later and having dinner together. I'm sure he was simply being polite."

"Did it feel simply polite?"

"It felt a bit flirtatious," Abigail admitted. "He winked when he said it."

"And did you see him later?"

"No, not at all. He left with his keys, and I went back to my box of papers. I didn't finish the box until nearly four o'clock. By the time I ran everything I didn't want through the shredder and then tidied up a bit, it was nearly five. I went over to the kitchen and spent some time with Marcia, mostly talking, but I did peel a few potatoes as well. Then I had dinner with her before I went back to the office and tackled another box."

"Is that what you typically do in the evenings?"

"When we have guests, I prefer to be at the front desk as much as possible," Abigail explained. "Even though Mr. Morris was staying in the annex, if he'd had any questions or concerns, he'd have probably come to the front desk. I thought I should be there."

"What happened next?"

"I stayed at the desk until just after ten before I forwarded the phones and went back to my room."

"In the annex."

"Yes, in the annex."

"And you didn't see Mr. Morris when you went back to the annex?"

"I didn't see anyone. I also didn't see Mr. Morris's car. I never saw it, actually, but he wrote what he was driving on his registration card."

"I'm going to need a copy of that card."

"No problem."

"Were there any lights on in Mr. Morris's room when you went back to your room?"

Abigail shook her head. "I did look, but his room was dark, and there weren't any cars parked anywhere near it."

"And then you let yourself into your room and went to bed?"

"Yes, with an alarm set for seven. I heard at least one car drive past the annex during the night, but I didn't pay any attention. I just assumed that it was Mr. Morris, coming back from wherever he'd been."

"You didn't notice the time?"

"I can't really see the clock on my bedside table without squinting or putting on my glasses. I didn't bother doing either of those things last night. If Mr. Morris hadn't been staying here, I probably would have gotten up and checked to see who was driving around the grounds in the middle of the night."

"What happened today, then?"

"I got up at seven and had breakfast with Marcia and Carl. Marcia told me that she hadn't seen our guest, and we laughed about how nice it was to have guests who didn't eat the meals that were included in their room rate. Then I went back to the desk and spent a frustrating morning trying to get the website working. After lunch, I decided to give all of the annex rooms a good clean." She stopped and then shrugged. "I timed myself while I was working. I'm trying to work out how long it's going to take me to clean the rooms once we start having guests. I timed how long it took to clean an empty room, and I was looking forward to seeing how much more time it took to clean 2A after Mr. Morris left."

"What time is checkout?"

"We ask our guests to leave by noon. I gave Mr. Morris some extra time while I cleaned the other rooms, but when he hadn't appeared by two, I decided to let myself into his room. I thought that maybe he'd gone and just left his key in the room. Jack and Janet said people used to do that all the time."

"But he hadn't."

"No," Abigail said sadly. "He hadn't."

Chapter Three

A n hour later, Abigail felt as if she'd repeated everything she knew at least a dozen times. She'd given Fred a copy of the registration card that Mr. Morris had completed and then watched from behind the reception desk as he'd gone back outside to the annex. As soon as the door shut behind him, she reached for her cell.

Call me when you can. It isn't exactly an emergency, but it's close.

Her cell rang two minutes later.

"What's wrong?" her sister, Mandy, demanded.

"You know that man I texted you about last night?"

"The unexpected guest who talked you into letting him stay?"

"Yeah, him. Well, he didn't check out this morning, so I finally let myself into his room."

"And he'd completely trashed it? Please don't tell me that he turned it into a meth lab or a porn studio or something."

"You have an overactive imagination, although either of those things would be preferable to the truth."

"Seriously? What happened?"

"I found his body."

There was a long silence on the phone.

"Hello?"

"Sorry, but did you just say what I thought you said?"

"If you thought I said that I found his body, then yes."

Mandy blew out a sigh. "I suppose people die every day, but it still must have been horrible for you. Do you think he had a heart attack? Did you have to call the police?"

"He didn't have a heart attack. At least, I don't think he had a heart attack. There was a lot of blood."

"He killed himself? Oh, Abby, I'm sorry."

Abigail thought for a moment. "I suppose it's possible that he killed himself, but the police are treating it as a murder investigation."

After another extended silence, Mandy spoke again. "I'm not often left speechless, and that's twice in a single conversation. Murder?"

"Like I said, there was a lot of blood."

"Do you need me?"

"Aren't you terribly busy?"

"We're building sets all week. I've been working with the lead designer. He's done several Broadway shows and he's amazing, but if you need me, I'll tell him I need a few days off."

"And then you'll get fired."

Mandy sighed. "That's always a possibility. The show opens in six weeks, and we have an awful lot to do between now and then."

"Then you can't come here, even if I want you here."

"Except my sister is more important to me than any job. I'll come if you need me."

"I don't need you," Abigail said firmly. "When you took

that job, we agreed that I'd handle things here. I'm handling things."

"But murder? Neither of us saw that coming."

"No, neither did Mr. Morris, I'm sure."

Mandy sighed. "I have to get back to work. I'm hiding in the bathroom right now, but someone will notice I'm gone if I don't get back out there. I'll call you tonight, okay?"

"Okay, you get back to your dream job and I'll get back to, well, whatever this is."

"Love you, Big Sis."

"Love you, Little Sis."

Abigail pushed the button to end the call and then dropped the phone on the desk. "Whatever this is," she muttered to herself as she watched a police car roll slowly past the front window. She closed her eyes and then quickly opened them again as the memory of what she'd seen in room 2A flooded back to her.

"Work," she told herself sternly, reaching over to switch on the old computer. It was whirring and clunking to life when the front door opened.

"Hello?" Abigail said questioningly as a woman walked into the room.

The new arrival was tall, with grey hair pulled back in a loose ponytail. Her clothes were stylish and looked expensive. Although she was using a cane, she didn't seem to be relying on it for assistance as she strode into the lodge's lobby.

"Good afternoon," the woman replied with a smile. "Although it's really evening, isn't it? The day has simply flown past."

Abigail glanced at the clock. "It's already seven o'clock," she said. "I had no idea."

"And you probably didn't have any dinner, did you?"

"Uhm, no," Abigail said, surprised by the question.

"You must take proper care of yourself no matter how stressful life becomes," the woman told her.

"I suppose so," Abigail replied slowly. "But can I help you?"

"Oh, my goodness. I haven't even introduced myself," the woman laughed. "I'm Jessica Fleming. Everyone calls me Jessica, aside from the people who call me mom or granny, that is. I live right next door, and I would have come over and introduced myself the day you arrived, but I wasn't here. I've only just come back from spending time with my son and then my daughter."

"How nice for you."

Jessica nodded. "It was lovely. I hadn't been to a wedding in ages."

"A wedding?"

"Oh, yes, I left that part out. My son, Jason, got married for the first time at the age of fifty-three."

"Congratulations."

"Yes, thank you. I never thought he'd get married, not after all this time. Of course, for many years, he simply couldn't get married, but he and his partner have been together since they met in college. Even after it became possible, Jason and Brian both agreed that they were happy with their relationship just the way it was. They didn't want to complicate things, and they didn't think that being married would make their relationship any better."

"A lot of people seem to feel that way these days."

"And I've never been one to tell my children what to do with their lives, so I stayed out of it. You can imagine how surprised I was when Jason called and told me that he and Brian were planning a wedding. One of their friends convinced them that they should finally take the plunge."

"Good for them."

"I think it will be, actually, for all sorts of reasons. They were both incredibly happy during the wedding weekend. We laughed and talked and danced and drank and ate amazing food. I don't remember the last time I had so much fun. And then they left for their honeymoon. They're spending a month touring Europe together."

"That sounds like a wonderful honeymoon."

"Jason speaks reasonably good Spanish and Brian has a basic grasp of French, so of course, they headed straight to Italy," Jessica laughed. "I told them they should at least start where they could speak the language, but they wanted to do things their own way. They're having a wonderful time despite the language barriers."

"Good for them. I've always wanted to travel around Europe. Maybe one day."

"They travel quite a lot, actually. They live in Boston, which means they can fly from there to just about anywhere. They're both very sensible with money, and they both have good jobs, so they can afford to travel regularly."

"You must be very proud of your son."

Jessica flushed. "I'm incredibly proud of both Jason and Brian. Jason is a history professor at a college in Boston, and Brian is head of the department of mechanical engineering at the same school. He has three patents for some sort of special screw that attaches to a bolt or nut or something in a special way. He came up with the idea years ago and worked with a group of students at the college to design it. He has another team working on some other sort of fastener now, and he thinks the new one will be even better than the old one."

"Wow. That's very cool."

"The original design is used in cars all around the world. You probably have some in your car right now."

"How long were you in Boston?"

"I was there for just over a week. I went a few days before the wedding and then stayed and did some sightseeing on my own after the wedding. Once I'd seen everything I wanted to see, I went and spent ten days with my daughter."

"Where does your daughter live?"

"Julia is in DC. She works for the government as some sort of analyst. She has a PhD in mathematics, and she actually enjoys things like calculus."

"Good for her. I'm afraid I struggled with my business math classes and had no interest in taking calculus."

"In my day, women weren't encouraged to study math, science, or engineering. We were supposed to be teachers or nurses. I got a teaching degree, because that was what was expected of me, but then I got married and had children and never actually taught. Once the children were a bit older, I went to work for my husband, helping him run the family manufacturing business. I did that until he passed away nearly thirty years ago."

"I'm sorry for your loss."

Jessica shrugged. "Thomas was a good man and a good husband and father. It sounds terrible to say that I was never madly in love with him, but I married him because he asked, expecting that I would come to love him eventually. We had a good marriage and two wonderful children together, but once he was gone, I realized that I'm actually happier on my own. I had all sorts of ideas that I wanted to explore with the business, ideas that Thomas would never have entertained, but that didn't work out."

"Oh?"

"Thomas had been left fifty percent of the company by his father. There were five cousins who each owned ten percent. Their father was Thomas's father's brother. Anyway, after Thomas died, one of the cousins decided that he should take over the day-to-day management of the company. I'd been running things for years by that point, but Theodore managed to persuade his brothers and sisters that he should take over. I could have fought them about it, but it was easier to simply sell Thomas's share of the business to them. At that point, the company was very successful and the payout they gave me meant that I could essentially retire and not worry about money ever again."

"How nice for you."

"It took Theodore only five years to run the company out of business. I was the only one who wasn't at all surprised," Jessica told her.

"What a shame."

"I still had some connections in the business world, so I helped the people who worked there find other jobs. Theodore and his siblings tried to sue me to get back some of the money they'd paid me for my share of the business, but the valuation that had been used for the sale was solid, and I'd used an excellent lawyer. They couldn't do anything besides complain bitterly to the rest of the family."

"So what happened to Theodore?" Abigail had to ask.

"Oh, I helped him find another job, too. He was a hard worker, and he'd been a real asset to the company while Thomas had been alive, but he really wasn't capable of running the business. He ended up working for what had been one of their biggest competitors until he finally retired just before he turned seventy."

"It was kind of you to help him after everything that had happened."

"He was family. Okay, he was Thomas's family and not mine. I only talk about my own family when I've been drinking."

Abigail raised an eyebrow. "Really?"

Jessica laughed. "I'm seventy-five years old, and I still haven't fully recovered from my rather unpleasant childhood. I did my best to give my own children something better."

"It sounds as if you managed it."

"And then Julia did an amazing job bringing up her own daughter, Jennifer, in spite of very difficult circumstances."

"So you have a granddaughter."

"I do. I encouraged both of my children to wait to get married until they found someone they felt they couldn't live without. I've already told you that Jason waited a good deal longer, but Julia fell madly in love when she was in her early twenties. She was still in school, working on her doctorate at the time while holding down a full-time job. Will worked in the same office and they quickly became inseparable."

"Why do I feel as if this story doesn't have a happy ending?"

Jessica sighed. "They were living together and talking about getting engaged when Julia found out that she was pregnant. She was not terribly pleased, but Will was thrilled. He proposed immediately, and they started planning a small ceremony within a few months. Sadly, Will died in a plane crash before they could follow through on their plans."

"How awful for your daughter."

"It was a very difficult time for her. She very nearly dropped out of school, and she did quit her job because everything there reminded her of Will. Fortunately, Will's parents were incredibly supportive. He was their only child and they wanted to do everything they could to ensure that they would be a part of their only grandchild's life. His father passed away ten years ago, but Julia is still close to Will's mother, and Jennifer grew up spending half of her summer with them and the other half with me."

"And what does Jennifer do?"

"She has a doctorate in biomedical engineering and works for a biotech company that's working on using nanotechnology for drug delivery. And yes, that is exactly, word for word, what she told me when I asked her to tell me about her job."

Abigail laughed. "It sounds very impressive."

"She loves it. She also has a boyfriend, but she isn't particularly interested in getting married. She just celebrated her thirtieth birthday by taking a cruise with three of her best girlfriends from her college days. Women get to have much more interesting lives now than they did when I was young."

"I don't know that my life is all that interesting," Abigail told her. "I'm excited about my new business, but I haven't had a chance to make any new friends in the area yet."

"Did you leave a boyfriend or girlfriend back in the city?"

"I left a few friends of both genders, but not a romantic partner. Maybe I'll find the man of my dreams in Nightshade."

"There are a number of eligible men around your age here. I'll have to see what I can do. Jack and Janet told me all about you and your sister and about how delighted they were that you were buying the lodge, of course. I'm happy to finally meet you, even under these less-than-ideal circumstances."

"It's nice to meet you, too. Did I give you my name? I'm Abigail Clark."

"Yes, of course, and your sister is Amanda. Where is she?"

Abigail sighed. "She's still in New York City. Just before we were due to move, she was offered a wonderful job that she simply couldn't turn down."

"How nice for her, but how difficult for you."

"It's fine. I was going to be managing the hotel anyway. Mandy was going to be in charge of coming up with themes for the cottages and then supervising their renovations."

"And Jack and Janet had some wonderful staff. I assume you've kept them all. You'd be crazy to have let any of them go."

Abigail flushed. "I've kept them all. They've all been a big help thus far."

Jessica nodded. "I hope you don't mind if I sit down," she said as she headed toward one of the couches.

"Oh, goodness, of course not. Please, sit." Abigail jumped up and walked across to where Jessica was slowly lowering herself onto a couch.

"Thank you, dear. Now if I just had a cup of tea, I'd be perfectly happy."

"Tea? I suppose – that is, I could, uhm, I don't know."

"Janet had one of those machines that makes tea and coffee from pods right at the reception desk. Don't tell me she took it with her."

Abigail looked at the desk and then back at her guest. "She must have, because it isn't there any longer. I should get another one, really. It would be good to be able to offer tea and coffee to our guests throughout the day."

"Yes, well, never mind. For now, just sit down and tell me what's happening in the annex. I went out after lunch to get some shopping done, and when I came back there were dozens of police cars everywhere."

Abigail sighed. "I don't know what I'm allowed to tell anyone."

Jessica waved a hand. "Then I'll tell you what I know. I've lived in Nightshade my entire life, and I have friends everywhere. Before I came over, I made a few phone calls. While murder is always shocking, I wasn't all that surprised to hear that Rusty Morris was the victim."

Abigail's jaw dropped. "You knew Mr. Morris?"

Jessica grinned at her. "Everyone in Nightshade knew Rusty Morris. He used to live here, years ago, but he moved away, well, it must have been nine or ten years ago now. Maybe a bit more, actually."

"He didn't mention that when he arrived."

"All things considered, that isn't surprising. What is surprising is that he wasn't on Jack and Janet's blacklist."

"Blacklist?"

"Didn't they give you a list of names of people you should turn away? After all their years in business, they must have built up a substantial list."

Abigail frowned. "They didn't give me anything like that."

"How unfortunate for you. Well, if they had, Rusty Morris would have been on the top of the list."

"Why? He seemed quite nice – charming, even."

Jessica laughed. "Charming is the perfect word for him. He was exactly that, which was part of the problem. He came into town and charmed everyone with stories about the business he was going to start here. He managed to persuade half the town to invest in his plans for grand restorations at the Xanzibar Hotel and then ran away with the money without ever even taking a look at the property."

"The Xanzibar Hotel?"

"Xanzibar with an X for some reason or another. You can see it from the lodge's dock. It's the big building at the opposite end of Foxglove Lake, near the lighthouse. It was built in the eighties as a luxury hotel, and it proved very popular for a few summers before people got tired of it and started vacationing elsewhere. It stayed open for a few more years, but it's been sitting empty ever since."

"I did notice the building, but I assumed it was a private residence. Is it for sale?"

"If you get a bit closer to it, you'll quickly realize that it's far too large to be a private home. As for whether it's for sale or not, I wish I knew. Herb and Tammy Fuhrman were the original owners. Herb inherited the Fuhrman family fortune. At one point, the family owned at least half of Nightshade, but his father wasted a lot of money on projects that never actually came to fruition. At one point, he started building an amusement park, but costs skyrocketed, and it was never finished. When he died, Herb took over, and for a while it seemed as if he was going to do a better job of managing the family business."

"But that didn't happen?"

"Things seemed to be going well until Herb decided to build the Nightshade Hotel. That was what he called it, and he poured a lot of money into the building. The whole town watched in awe as he had marble flooring flown in from Italy, chandeliers brought in from somewhere else, and hand-carved furniture custom-made for each guest room. Herb had a long list of Hollywood celebrities at the grand opening celebration, but the hotel hadn't even been open for a month before it was sold, and the name was changed. We were all surprised, because it seemed to be doing really well, but the Nightshade Hotel became the Xanzibar Hotel overnight."

"So who owns it now, and what does it have to do with Rusty Morris?" Abigail asked.

"No one knows who bought the property. Oh, the sale was public knowledge, of course, but the Fuhrmans sold it to a company called Nightshade Industries, and no one I know has any idea who owns Nightshade Industries. No one has been able to find out, either."

"How interesting."

"As I said before, the hotel stayed open for a few years and then shut without warning. When Rusty arrived in town, he claimed that he knew the owners and that he was working with them to purchase the property. We never should have believed him, but we were all excited to hear that something might finally be done with the place. And Rusty had big ideas and tons of enthusiasm. He convinced us that he could attract all sorts of wealthy guests and that he could rent it out as a movie set and for television shows and all sorts."

"So Rusty got people to give him money?"

"He got just about everyone to give him money. Some of us only gave him a few hundred dollars, but that was enough to get us a worthless certificate that said we owned part of Rusty's new company, Morris Hospitality, Incorporated."

"How much money are we talking about?"

"After he left, the local paper estimated that he'd gotten away with at least half a million dollars."

Chapter Four

Abigail whistled. "That's a lot of money."

"Indeed. As I said, I only gave him a couple of hundred dollars, but I know a lot of people who gave him quite a bit more. Jack and Janet gave him ten thousand dollars. They were hopeful that the reopening of the Xanzibar would bring more tourists to Nightshade, some of whom would end up staying here when the Xanzibar was full. Some of the other local businesses were even more eager to see the Xanzibar reopen and gave Rusty even larger sums of money," Jessica told her.

"And then he simply disappeared with the money?"

Jessica nodded. "He had a big fundraising event here at Sunset Lodge. There were bounce houses for the kids and food and entertainment. Everyone was happy to turn up to support the event because Rusty had promised to hire locals to do every bit of work that needed doing at the hotel. You can imagine how exciting that was for our local construction companies, contractors, plumbers, electricians, and so on. We all thought it was Christmas, really, right up until the day after the fundraiser."

"When Rusty disappeared."

"Yup. The big event had concluded with a few fireworks, and then we'd all gone home to dream of what life was going to be like around here once the Xanzibar was attracting rich and famous guests. Rusty got up the next morning and had breakfast with Janet before telling her that he needed to go to New York City for a few days to talk to his lawyers and what-not. It wasn't until a week or so later that we started to worry that he wasn't coming back."

"Couldn't you have had him arrested?"

"Some people talked to the police, but apparently there wasn't really anything they could do. We'd all signed contracts when we bought our shares in Rusty's company, contracts that stated very clearly that there were risks involved in the investment and that the money could be used by Rusty in whatever way he wanted to use it. It was all in very tiny print, of course, but regardless, we trusted Rusty, right up until he left."

"And you never saw him again?"

"As far as I know, he never came back."

"Until yesterday."

Jessica nodded. "I wonder what brought him back to Nightshade."

"I suppose that's the first thing the police are going to try to work out. Whatever brought him here got him killed, after all."

"Maybe, or maybe someone just spotted him on the street and followed him back here and killed him," Jessica suggested. "Just about everyone in Nightshade hated him."

"Just about everyone?"

"There are probably a few people who managed to avoid his slick sales pitch all those years ago, and there are a handful of people who've moved to the town in the years since, but even those two groups of people will have friends or family members who were swindled by the man. I'm surprised he had the nerve to come back here, really."

"I don't envy the police. It sounds as if there are hundreds of people with a motive for the man's murder."

"Of course, some have a stronger motive than others. If I were Fred, I'd start with Lisa Carter and her husband."

"Oh? Who's Lisa Carter?"

"Rusty's former girlfriend. Not only did she invest every penny she had in his fake company, but she was also three months pregnant with Rusty's child when Rusty drove away from Nightshade."

"My goodness. The poor woman."

Jessica nodded. "I think Huey is ten now, or nearly. He's Huey Carter, after his stepfather, although I'm not certain that Huey knows that Ken Carter isn't his biological father."

"Ken Carter?"

"He married Lisa when she was nine months pregnant. She was practically in labor as she waddled down the aisle, but Ken didn't care. He'd been crazy in love with Lisa since they'd been in kindergarten together. They dated all through school, but then Lisa went away to college, and Ken stayed here to work on his father's farm. After she graduated, Lisa stayed in Pittsburgh until her mother got sick. She came back to Nightshade only a few days before Rusty Morris arrived."

"And then she fell in love with him."

"They met in the grocery store, of all places. Lisa was shopping for her mother. I'm not certain what Rusty was doing there, as he was staying here, but everyone in town heard about how they met in the bakery and how Rusty walked all the way around the entire store with her. She told me later that she was already halfway to falling in love with him by the time they reached the checkouts. He paid for her shopping and got her to agree to have dinner with him that night, and Rusty started spending most of his nights at her apartment a few days later."

"My goodness."

"A few people made comments, of course, but Lisa didn't care. She was crazy about Rusty, and he seemed to be equally devoted to her. I talked to her here, at the fundraiser the night before Rusty left. I mentioned that she looked quite tired, and she told me about the baby. She was really excited, and she said that Rusty was looking forward to becoming a father. According to Lisa, they were talking about getting married and planning to buy a house together."

"How could anyone abandon someone in that way?"

"As I said earlier, it wasn't until Rusty had been gone for a few days that people started to worry. Lisa held out hope that he'd come back for a lot longer than anyone else, but even she gave up toward the end of her pregnancy. Like I said, she married Ken Carter just before she had the baby."

"I hope they're happy together."

"Ken's a good man who works incredibly hard to support the family with his farm. Lisa's mom is still around, but she needs a lot of care. Lisa looks after her and also Huey and the two children she and Ken have together. The littlest one finally started school this year, and the last time I talked to Lisa she was enjoying a trip around the grocery store all by herself for the first time in a long time."

"I wonder if she knew that Rusty was in town."

"If she did, then she'll probably be a suspect in his murder," Jessica suggested. "Although, I think I'd suspect Ken more than Lisa. I can see him being worried that Lisa might leave him and run away with Rusty, given the opportunity."

"Surely Lisa would never have trusted Rusty again after the way he'd treated her."

"I'd like to think not, but the one thing I remember most about Rusty was how charming and persuasive he could be.

He talked me into investing with him, and I'm usually incredibly careful with my money. If anyone could have come up with a convincing story to persuade Lisa to give him another chance, it was Rusty Morris."

Abigail frowned. "I hope Ken has a solid alibi for last night. And I hope there are lots of other suspects. I haven't met Lisa or Ken yet, but I really don't want either of them to have been behind Rusty's murder."

"Oh, there are plenty of other suspects," Jessica assured her. "I would imagine that anyone who invested in Rusty's company will be on the list, but some people will be higher on the list than others."

"Who would you put at the top of the list, aside from Lisa and Ken?"

"If I were Fred, I'd be looking at some of the people who lost the most money to the man. I think Scott Wright invested quite a bit – but then, he could afford to lose it, too."

"Scott Wright?"

"You haven't met Scott yet? I would have thought he'd have been on your doorstep the day you arrived. Maybe he's in Paris or London or some other exotic place."

"Does he travel often?"

"He travels when he feels like traveling. If I were him, I'd travel all the time, but he seems to prefer staying in Nightshade most of the time. I suppose he's busy counting his money most days." Jessica held up a hand. "I'm being unfair. He did inherit a fortune, but he also works quite hard to keep his businesses successful."

"What businesses?"

"Here in Nightshade, Scott owns the Lakeside Restaurant, Charlie's Bar and Grill, Cakes and More Bakery, and both of the strip plazas in town. As Herb Fuhrman slowly sold off everything he owned over the last ten years, Scott bought all of the most profitable properties. Besides what he owns here, I believe he owns at least a dozen other properties throughout the area."

"My goodness. That's a lot to manage."

"He has a team of people who help him. Scott's family owns property all over the Finger Lakes region. I was told that his father gave him a million dollars when he graduated from college and told him that that was all he was ever going to get, so he'd better invest it wisely."

"Surely he could have put the money in the bank and simply gotten a job," Abigail suggested.

"Maybe, but I can't see Scott working for someone else. He's been buying and selling businesses in the area for over twenty years now, and he's built up a reputation for making smart choices when buying properties and for being a good manager once he owns a business. I dare say investing with Rusty was one of only a few bad choices he's made in life."

"I wonder why he didn't buy Sunset Lodge."

"He looked at it, but Jack and Janet really wanted to sell the property to someone who would move in and run the place themselves. If Scott had bought it, he would have hired a team of managers to run the place, and it would have just become part of his portfolio. That wasn't what Jack and Janet wanted for the place they loved."

"And he isn't interested in buying the Xanzibar?"

"I think he might be, but he doesn't know anything about the owners. When Rusty turned up, claiming to be ready to purchase the place, I think Scott was just happy to invest in the deal."

"Why did you say you thought that Scott would have already introduced himself to me?"

"Because small businesses in small towns all have to work together to support one another. He'll be full of good ideas for ways you can work together for everyone's benefit."

Abigail nodded. "Jack and Janet mentioned that the businesses in the area all try to help one another – even the ones that might be considered competitors. I wasn't too worried about that, as we're the only place offering lodging in all of Nightshade."

"At least until someone buys the Xanzibar."

"Do you think that's possible?"

Jessica shrugged. "Yesterday I would have said no, but the fact that Rusty was back in town makes me wonder. Maybe he came back now because he was finally able to start moving forward with the purchase."

"Would that make Scott want to kill him?"

"Oh, goodness, I have no idea. The only reason I suggested Scott as a suspect is because I know he invested quite a lot in Rusty's business. For all I know, Rusty paid him back, or maybe what I think of as a large amount is only spare change to Scott. I can't imagine Scott will be a serious suspect in the murder, but, having said that, I also can't imagine who would be. Not really."

"Aside from Lisa and Ken Carter."

"I don't know. The more I think about it, the harder it is for me to imagine anyone I know killing anyone. I'm sure Lisa hated him for what he did to her, and I'm sure that Ken hated him for hurting Lisa, but the jump from hate to murder is a big one, one that I can't see either of them making."

"So who do you think might have killed Rusty?"

"That's the big question, isn't it? I would imagine everyone in Nightshade is asking that question right now. I suppose if Dr. Cooper had done it, he'd have found a way to kill the man without it looking like murder."

"Dr. Cooper?"

"Mark Cooper, Nightshade's most popular family doctor. He's also Nightshade's only family doctor, but we all love him. He's wonderful with patients of all ages."

"But you think he had a motive for killing Rusty Morris?"

"I know he invested some money with Rusty, but the reason he came to mind is because Dr. Cooper's wife also invested money with Rusty. Quite a lot of money, actually. There were rumors at the time that she and Rusty were very close, if you know what I mean."

"I thought he and Lisa were devoted to one another," Abigail protested, feeling a bit overwhelmed.

Jessica shrugged. "They seemed happy together whenever I saw them anywhere, but that didn't stop the rumors about Rusty and more than one married woman in town."

"Oh, dear. That will give Fred even more suspects to consider."

"Actually, I heard rumors about three different married women being involved with Rusty during the months he was here. Two of those women have since left Nightshade, one with her husband and the other on her own. Her husband left town not long after, though. Mark Cooper is the only one who is still here."

"What about his wife?"

"Oh, I missed that part out of the story. Sharon died a few months after Rusty left town. She was on her way to Canada to visit friends when she lost control of her car on an icy road and crashed into an oncoming truck."

"How awful."

"It was quite sad. Dr. Cooper was terribly upset, of course. He took some time off and went and stayed with his parents for a few months. We were all worried that he wasn't going to come back, but he eventually did."

Abigail sighed. "So whether she had an affair with the man or not, they both lost money to Rusty."

"Yes, and Sharon gave him nearly every penny she had. She'd inherited tens of thousands of dollars when her grandmother died, and she gave all of that money to Rusty. That was part of what made everyone so suspicious about her relationship with the man, of course. I heard that Dr. Cooper was furious about it. He'd already given Rusty an investment by that point, one that he and Sharon had agreed they could afford. I don't think he was expecting her to go behind his back to invest even more."

"With what Rusty did to the people of Nightshade, I'm not sure how the police are going to narrow down the list of suspects. Besides the people we've already discussed, is there anyone else who you think might have had a motive other than the money that Rusty stole?"

"That money seems like a pretty strong motive to me, but I did wonder about Tom Evans when I first heard who'd been killed."

"Who is Tom Evans?"

"Haven't you met Tom yet? You'll meet him once you start planning to have work done around here. He's a contractor, and if you need one, he's the only one you should consider using. He works with the best electricians, plumbers, carpenters, whatever you need, in the area, and he gets them to give him the best possible prices. He's also a nice man who happens to be around your age and single."

"If he's so wonderful, why is he on your list of suspects?"

Jessica frowned. "He worked closely with Rusty when Rusty was here. At the time, I would have called them friends, if anyone had asked. Rusty told everyone that he was going to use Tom for all of the work that needed to be done at the Xanzibar. After Rusty left, Tom insisted that he'd been as taken in as the rest of us. He claimed that he'd invested some of his own money in Rusty's company and that he'd put off other jobs because he thought he was going to be working on the Xanzibar."

"Anyone else?"

Jessica sighed. "Do you have a local telephone directory?"

"I'm not sure. Maybe."

"Janet kept one in the drawer at the reception desk."

Abigail crossed the room and then opened the drawer. She nearly missed the thin booklet that didn't look like a telephone directory to her.

"'The Nightshade Residential Directory,'" she read off the cover. The words were difficult to read against the bright floral print design that had made the booklet look more like a guide to gardening than anything else.

"That's the one. Now you can sit down and go through Fred's list of suspects from beginning to end."

Abigail opened the book and read the first name on the list.

"Lost about five hundred dollars to Rusty," Jessica told her.

"What about Annie Abrams? Or Ira Adams? Or Horace Bates?" Abigail asked, choosing names at random from the first page.

"Ira invested two hundred and twelve dollars in Rusty's business. I know the exact amount because he reminds me of it every time he sees me. He seems to think that I encouraged him to invest, but I don't remember it that way. As for Annie, she wasn't living in Nightshade when Rusty was here, but Horace gave him some money. I don't know how much, but he took it out of what was supposed to be his son's college fund. His wife was furious, but in the end, their son didn't want to go to college anyway. He joined the Navy and spends his time in a submarine now."

"Do you really think that Fred is going to go through the telephone directory and try to speak to everyone who lost money to Rusty?"

Jessica shrugged. "I have no idea how the police investigate murders. If the only motive was the money that Rusty stole, then nearly everyone in that book had a motive. Fred needs to hope that there was more to it than that. Or maybe the killer left fingerprints or dropped his or her wallet or something. The case may already be solved."

"Oh, I hope so. I hate the thought that there's a killer walking around Nightshade."

"Don't we all?" Jessica replied.

Chapter Five

Jessica stayed for a short while longer, chatting with Abigail about the lodge and Nightshade. After she left, Abigail found herself feeling restless and anxious.

"A man was murdered just a few doors away from where I was sleeping," she told her reflection as she brushed her shoulder-length brown hair. "I really hope the police have already worked out who killed him. I may not sleep again until I know the killer is behind bars."

She made a face at herself in the mirror and then sighed and walked back out into the lodge's lobby. A noise behind her made her jump and spin around, her heart racing.

"Good afternoon," Carl Young said as he shuffled toward her. "I hope I didn't startle you."

"I'm just a bit on edge," Abigail admitted. "And I didn't know you were there."

"I was working my way through the list you gave me, but the next thing on the list is checking all of the plumbing in the annex. I walked over there, but the police wouldn't let me anywhere near the building."

Abigail frowned. "I hope they'll let me into my room later.

If they don't want me to sleep out there, I'll have to pack a bag and move in here."

"I think that might be wise. I suspect the police are going to be working all through the night out there. They were setting up some big lights when I walked past."

"Big lights? Oh, great."

"I suppose they're looking for clues. As far as I'm concerned, whoever killed that man did the world a favor, and I told Fred Williams that, too."

"I'm not sure you should say those sorts of things to the police during a murder investigation."

Carl shrugged. "I invested five hundred dollars in Rusty Morris's business, and I got exactly nothing in return. I'd been saving that money to take myself on a little vacation one day, and it took me another eighteen months to replace the money."

"Where did you go on your vacation?"

"That time I went to New York City and went to some Broadway shows. I like to go different places every few years, but I never go too far away."

Abigail nodded. "Does everyone in Nightshade know about the murder and the victim, then?"

"Everyone is talking about it. Fred wasn't very happy when he questioned me that I already knew who was dead, but you can't keep a secret that big in a town this small. I imagine the whole town will turn up at the funeral, just to be certain that the miserable thief is truly dead."

"If news travels that fast, who knew when he arrived in town?"

Carl shrugged. "I wish I'd known. I'd have loved to punch him in the face."

"But you didn't find out he was here until after he was dead?"

"No one was talking about Rusty Morris yesterday," Carl

told her. "We were all still bitter and angry, but he was old news, and there wasn't any point in bringing him up – not unless you wanted to upset everyone in the room."

"Someone clearly knew he was here."

"I knew we had a guest in the annex, but I never saw him. I'm not sure Fred believed me when I told him that, though."

"I never saw him again after he checked in. He said something about seeing me at dinner, but he didn't come to the dining room while I was there, and Marcia told me at breakfast that he hadn't come in after I left, either."

"He probably didn't want anyone to see him. If Marcia had known he was here, she would have told everyone in town."

"Did she lose money to him?"

"Everyone lost money to him," Carl said bitterly. "Marcia and Howard invested something. I'm not sure how much, but I know Howard was furious when Rusty disappeared. He filed a police report and tried to hire a lawyer to file a lawsuit, but Quail wouldn't take the case."

"Quail?"

"Quail is one of Nightshade's finest lawyers. He's one of our only lawyers, truth be told, but he's pretty good, and he's more honest than most. He's one of the partners in Duncan, Duncan, and Duncan, the only law firm in Nightshade."

"Duncan, Duncan, and Duncan? Is his last name Duncan, then?"

"It is, yes. He's the oldest Duncan. His sister, Dove, came next, and the youngest brother is Hawk. Their father was a lawyer in Buffalo, where they grew up. When Quail graduated from law school, he decided to start his own firm in a small town. Apparently, he considered several different towns before he finally decided on Nightshade."

"And then his sister and brother joined him here?"

Carl nodded. "He thought, when he opened his doors

twenty years ago, that the town was just the right size for one lawyer, but it turned out that there's more than enough work for three."

"Really? Did any of the Duncans lose money to Rusty?"

"Nope. We all realized, after Rusty disappeared, that he'd done his best to avoid all of them. When Quail read the fine print on the contracts that we'd all signed, he could see why Rusty hadn't ever asked him for any money."

"But no one took the contract to Quail before signing it?"

Carl shrugged. "Some people probably thought about it, but Rusty seemed trustworthy, and he was clever, too. When I asked about having a lawyer look over the contract, he told me that if I was that concerned about the money, I shouldn't invest. He insisted that he didn't want to do business with anyone who didn't trust him enough to take him at his word." Carl flushed. "I was just dumb enough to fall for it."

"I spoke to him only briefly, but I thought he was charming," Abigail replied. "I can see how he managed to talk people into giving him money. He talked me into letting him stay here, even though we aren't supposed to be open, after all."

Carl grinned. "I did wonder, when you said we had a guest, why you'd agreed to let someone stay. I should have asked. If you'd told me who was here, I'd have chased Rusty Morris out of town."

"And probably saved his life," Abigail said sadly.

"Let's just hope Fred works out what happened quickly. Murders aren't good for business."

"I hadn't thought of that. I hope it doesn't discourage too many potential guests. I was hoping to start taking reservations soon."

"The winter months are always slow. I hope Jack and Janet didn't tell you otherwise."

"No, they were very honest about how quiet the lodge usually is from September to April. Mandy and I were hoping to find ways to attract guests, though. But maybe I should wait to start advertising until after the killer is behind bars."

"That's assuming Fred solves the murder," Carl said gloomily. "As far as I know, this is the first time he's ever had to investigate a murder."

"And it appears that he has a long list of possible suspects."

"Pretty much everyone in Nightshade, I would imagine," Carl agreed.

Abigail sighed. "Maybe it isn't too late for me to get my old job back."

"I hope you don't mean that."

"It's a tempting thought, but Mandy and I have sunk every penny we had into buying the lodge. We need to make it work."

"You know that Marcia and Arnold and I will do everything we can to help. We all love it here, and we really want you to succeed."

"Thank you so much," Abigail replied, feeling deeply touched by the words. "We should have a meeting, all four of us, to talk about what Mandy and I want to do in the weeks and months ahead. Let's plan to meet tomorrow afternoon. I was planning to have weekly staff meetings when I first arrived, but actually arranging them slipped down my to-do list because of, well, life."

Carl nodded. "What time?"

"Let's say one o'clock. That shouldn't interfere with Marcia's cooking or baking too much, I hope. I'll text both Marcia and Arnold now and invite them." She pulled out her phone and sent the messages.

"What do you want me to do now, then?" Carl asked as she put her phone down on the desk.

"I suppose you can skip checking the plumbing in the annex for today and move on to the next thing on the list. You may not be able to get into the annex rooms for a few days."

"I don't want to go into the room where the body was found ever, if I don't have to."

Abigail sighed. "I feel the same way, but I don't suppose I have much choice. Once the body is gone, I'll have to clean the room. I don't know that I'll ever have anyone stay there again, though."

Carl shivered. "You couldn't pay me enough to stay in that room. Okay, that's a lie. If you gave me a million dollars, I'd stay there, but only if the whole room had been cleaned from top to bottom and all of the furniture had been replaced."

"Maybe we'll just take all of the furniture out of that room and use it for storage once it's empty."

Carl opened his mouth to reply but shut it again as the front door swung open. Abigail smiled at the handsome man who walked into the lobby.

"Good afternoon," he said, nodding at Abigail. He looked somewhere in his early forties, with dark brown hair and lighter brown eyes. When he smiled at her, she felt her heart race.

"Good afternoon," she replied, wishing she'd checked her appearance more closely in the mirror earlier.

"Good afternoon, Dr. Cooper," Carl said.

The man turned his head and smiled at Carl. "Good afternoon, Carl. How are you today?"

"I'm good, thanks, Doc. My toe hasn't been giving me any more trouble," Carl replied.

"That's good to hear. It should be fine now, assuming you keep hammers away from it."

Carl chuckled. "I'm doing my best."

Dr. Cooper turned his attention back to Abigail. "I hope you don't mind my simply dropping in, but I wanted to introduce myself. I'm Mark Cooper, Nightshade's family doctor. Please call me Mark."

"It's very nice to meet you. I'm Abigail Clark."

"Jack and Janet told me all about you. I think everyone in town was delighted to hear that you and your sister were buying the lodge," the doctor replied as he walked toward the desk.

"I hope so. We're both excited to be a part of the community here."

"It's a wonderful community. I wasn't sure about it when I first moved here, but I've come to love it very much."

"I've been here only a few weeks, but so far everyone I've met has been very welcoming."

He nodded. "You may run into a few people in the area who won't be happy that you rented a room to Rusty Morris."

Abigail flushed. "I had no idea who he was when he arrived. I didn't find out about him until this afternoon when Jessica came to visit."

Mark grinned. "I'm sure Jessica had a lot to say about the man, but then everyone in Nightshade could probably tell you the entire sad story. Regardless of what the man did, he didn't deserve to be murdered."

"Of course not," Abigail agreed.

"He did deserve to be punched," Carl chimed in. "I wish I'd have had a chance to do that before he died."

"I think that if word had gotten out that he was here, there would have been a line halfway to Rochester full of people who wanted to punch the man," Mark replied. "I can't imagine why he came back to Nightshade. I don't suppose he told you anything about his plans for while he was here?"

Abigail frowned. "He said he was here for a meeting, but that was all that he said."

"What a shame. That will make Fred's job more difficult," Mark replied.

"I don't know that he's up to the job," Carl said. "Finding a killer is going to be a lot harder than finding the kids that stole a car for a joyride or working out who broke into the QuackMart for a case of beer after hours."

"QuackMart?" Abigail echoed.

Carl and Mark both laughed.

"It used to be QuickMart," Carl explained. "It was part of a chain in the area, but then they went out of business. When Scott Wright bought it, he didn't want to pay a fortune for new signs, so he just had the letter I replaced with a letter A and trademarked the name QuackMart."

"Scott Wright owns it?" Abigail asked.

"Scott owns at least a quarter of the town," Mark told her. "Besides QuackMart, he owns several restaurants, a boat rental company, a few strip plazas, and the ice cream factory."

"I haven't been to QuackMart, but I have seen the ice cream factory," Abigail replied.

"QuackMart is at the other end of the lake," Carl said. "It's right next to the old Xanzibar Hotel. From this side of the lake, we're closer to Wettermans."

"And that's where I've been getting all of my groceries," Abigail said. "They have a reasonable selection, and I've only needed snacks and some things for lunch, because Marcia takes care of breakfast and dinner every day."

Carl nodded. "I love Wettermans."

"Whereas I live near the middle of the lake, and I tend to shop at QuackMart," Mark said.

"What brought you here today?" Carl asked.

"Someone on the crime scene team managed to trip over a tree stump and land on his head. Fred insisted on having me come out to take a look at him, just in case he had a concussion," Mark explained.

"I hope he's okay," Abigail exclaimed.

"He's fine. I'm not sure how he managed it, but aside from some cuts and scrapes on his forehead and his knees, he's absolutely fine," Mark assured her.

"Which tree stump?" Carl wondered.

"I have no idea, but I would imagine it was one near the annex. Fred wouldn't let me get anywhere near the building, though. He had me examine the injured man in a parked car in the main parking lot," Mark replied.

"Don't they need a doctor to declare someone dead?" Abigail asked.

"Once it was clear that Rusty was dead, the state police will have brought in their own expert for that job," Mark explained. "If the ambulance crew had thought there was any chance that he was still alive, they'd have taken him to a hospital. I assume they could tell fairly easily that he was dead."

Abigail shuddered as the image of the man on the bed flashed through her head. "It was obvious," she said softly.

Mark put a hand on her arm. "I'm sorry," he said. "I didn't mean to bring back bad memories."

She shook her head. "It's fine."

"It isn't fine," Mark said. "You've had a huge shock. You may find that you have difficulty sleeping. If you start having nightmares or you simply can't sleep, please call me. I can give you something that would help for just a few days, until the worst of it starts to fade."

"Thank you," Abigail said.

Mark reached into his pocket and pulled out a small card case. He took out a business card and then picked up a pen from the desk and wrote something on the back of the card.

"Please don't hesitate to call me," he said as he put the card down in front of Abigail. "I've written my cell number on the back. I'd appreciate it if you don't share that with everyone in town, but I want you to have it. If you call the number on the front of the card, you'll get my answering service most of the time. I don't want you to have to deal with an extra step if you need any help."

"I'm sure I'll be fine," Abigail said as she picked up the card.

"If you need to talk to someone, I can help you find the right person to help you deal with what you saw," Mark continued. "I'm a doctor. I've seen dead bodies before. But I've never seen a murder victim, and I hope I never do."

Abigail shuddered. "I hope I never see another one. It was pretty awful."

"Was there a lot of blood?" Carl asked.

Mark held up a hand. "I'm pretty sure the police won't want that sort of information becoming public knowledge. I'm as curious as you are," he told Carl. "But it really isn't any of our business."

Carl shrugged. "I suspect every last detail will end up in the local paper. Ross has connections everywhere."

Mark nodded. "You're probably right. Have you met Ross?" he asked Abigail.

She shook her head.

"Ross Danielson owns the local paper, the *Nightshade News*. It comes out twice a week, on Wednesdays and Sundays," Mark explained. "He inherited the paper from his father, who'd inherited it from his father, back over a hundred years or so. I'm surprised Ross hasn't been to see you already, to ask you to buy some advertising."

Abigail frowned. "Now that you mention it, he's called a few times and left messages on the answering machine. I haven't called him back."

"He's probably out there," Carl said, gesturing toward the annex, "trying to get as much information as he can for his story. Rusty's murder will be the biggest story he's ever covered."

"I wonder if he'll have time to get it into tomorrow's paper," Mark said.

"No one buys the paper anymore," Carl replied. "He needs to put the story on the paper's website."

"I'm sure he will, once he gets done investigating," Mark said. "Ross does everything himself, from covering stories, to selling advertising, to running the website. The news sites in Buffalo and Rochester are probably already full of the news of Rusty's untimely demise, but Ross won't have had time to post anything yet."

Abigail sighed. "We really don't need bad publicity right now."

"You aren't ready for guests yet anyway," Carl reminded her. "Once Fred puts the killer behind bars, people will forget all about the murder in the annex."

"I hope you're right," Abigail replied.

"Hello, hello," a voice called as the door swung open again.

A pretty brunette stuck her head around the door. "I came as quickly as I could. I'm simply devastated, and this is the last place I want to be, but I couldn't stay away."

"Hello," Abigail replied, unable to think of a better response.

"I'm going to need a room for at least two nights," the woman told her as she crossed to the desk dragging a large suitcase behind her. "Maybe longer."

"We aren't actually open for business," Abigail replied. "There are several nice hotels nearby. I can give you a list."

The woman shook her head. "I have to stay here. You don't understand. I need to be as close as possible to where my husband died."

Chapter Six

"Your husband?" Abigail repeated.

"I'm Amy Morris," the woman told her. "I came as soon as I heard that Russ was dead." She shook her head. "We've only been married for just over a year. I can't really believe that he's gone, even though two policemen came and told me what had happened. After they left, I didn't know what to do, but after a while, it became clear to me. I needed to come here, to be as close to Russ as I possibly could be. I needed to see the things that he saw in his final hours. I, that is, oh..." She stopped talking and burst into tears.

"You've had a terrible shock," Mark said as he began to pat the woman's back.

She turned and then threw her arms around him and buried her head on his shoulder. "Please tell me it isn't true," she sobbed.

"I think you need to talk to the police," he replied, giving Abigail a slightly desperate look.

"Yes, someone needs to find Fred," Abigail replied.

"There, there," Mark said, awkwardly patting Amy's back.

Abigail found a box of tissues behind the desk and pulled them out. "Tissues," she announced loudly.

Amy lifted her head and stared at her. Abigail could see mascara stains across the shoulder of Mark's shirt.

"Here," she said, holding up the box.

Amy stared for a moment longer and then slowly reached out and took a tissue. As she wiped her eyes, Abigail looked at Mark. He was doing his best to put some distance between himself and the woman who was still clinging tightly to him.

"Let me get you a drink of water," Abigail said after a moment.

"I'll get it," Mark said loudly. "I know where to find everything in the kitchen. I used to spend a lot of time here with Jack and Janet." He backed away from Amy and disappeared behind the desk before Abigail could reply.

Amy took another tissue and patted her eyes gently. "I'm sure I'm a mess," she said softly.

"As Mark said, you've had a huge shock."

"Please tell me that you're going to let me stay here," Amy said, staring at Abigail as more tears filled her eyes.

"Yes, of course," Abigail replied against her better judgment.

"Excellent," Amy said. "I'd like the room next to the one where my husband was staying, please."

"That's going to be difficult," Carl muttered. When both women looked at him, he shrugged. "I should go and, um, check some pipes or something."

Abigail frowned as he nearly ran to the door.

"Where was Russ staying?" Amy asked, turning her attention back to Abigail.

"He requested a room in the annex. I'm afraid you can't stay out there, though."

"Why not?"

"The police are still working there. I'm fairly certain they won't want anyone staying out there. Actually, I'm not sure they'll want anyone staying here, either. I need to call the detective who interviewed me and see if I'm allowed to let you stay here or not."

"Surely the police can't stop you from running your business."

"But I did tell them that I wasn't going to be having any guests for the foreseeable future." *And I suspect they're going to want to talk to you, anyway,* she thought as she picked up her cell phone.

She found the card Fred had given her in her pocket and dialed the number he'd written on the back of it.

"Ah, yes, this is Abigail Clark."

"What can I do for you, Ms. Clark?"

"A guest has arrived, and I wasn't certain about letting her stay."

"That will be Amy Morris, will it? Mark Cooper called me from the kitchen to let me know that she'd just arrived."

Abigail felt a rush of gratitude toward the doctor. "Yes, that's right," she replied.

"I'm on my way to the lodge right now to speak with her," Fred told her. "Once I've had my chat with her, it's entirely up to you whether you rent her a room or not. She isn't going to be able to stay in the annex, but we can discuss that in a minute."

"Okay, great, thanks," Abigail said. She ended the call and put the phone down on the desk. "Detective Williams is on his way here," she told Amy. "We'll worry about where you can stay once he's had a chance to speak with you."

Amy sighed. "I've already talked to the police today. Unless he can tell me exactly what happened to Russ, I don't really want to talk to him."

"Sorry this took so long," Mark said as he walked back into the room carrying a glass of water. "My answering service called to let me know that one of my patients is in labor. She's on her way to the hospital now. I need to get over there."

He handed the glass to Amy, who gave him a huge smile. "Thank you so much for your kindness," she said.

"It was nice meeting you," he replied. "And you," he added, nodding at Abigail. "You know how to find me if you need me."

Abigail nodded. "Thanks for everything," she said.

"Just trying to help," he replied with a wink.

As he crossed to the door, it swung open, and Fred walked into the room. The two men exchanged greetings before Mark left. As the door shut behind him, Fred walked to the reception desk.

"Fred, this is Amy Morris, Russ's wife," Abigail said.

"Russ's widow," Amy said solemnly. "I have to keep reminding myself that he's dead. Otherwise I'll never believe it."

"Mrs. Morris, we weren't expecting you. I hope you don't mind that I have a few questions for you," Fred said gently.

Amy sighed. "I hope it's just a few. I already answered hundreds of questions from one of your colleagues earlier."

"Yes, so I've been told. You must have left home immediately after that conversation to have arrived here so quickly."

Amy flushed. "As soon as I heard what had happened, I knew I had to come here. I had to see what Russ had seen and talk to the people he'd spoken to in his final hours."

"Let's sit comfortably," Fred suggested, gesturing toward the couches on the opposite side of the room.

Abigail frowned as he escorted the woman across the room. *Mind your own business,* she told herself firmly. *But the murder happened here, so it is my business,* another voice argued. Sighing, she fired up the computer and then stared at the room assignment screen. *Where should I put the grieving widow?* she wondered as she scrolled through the options.

The cottages were out of the question. None of them were ready for guests. Whatever Fred thought, Abigail didn't like the idea of having Amy in the annex. That left the guest rooms in the main lodge. Feeling as if she couldn't charge the woman much under the circumstances, Abigail selected one of the smaller rooms on the second floor. After giving the matter some thought, she opted for a room that faced the front of the lodge, rather than one that looked out over the back. Giving Amy a room with a view of the annex seemed like a bad idea.

Fred and Amy walked back to the desk together a few minutes later.

"Please call me if you think of anything else that you think might help with the investigation," Fred told Amy.

She shrugged. "I don't know anything, but I'll keep your card, just in case."

Fred nodded. "Thank you." He turned to Abigail. "I'm going to ask you to come down to the annex with me and pack a bag. We'd like you to stay somewhere other than the annex for a few nights, while we're still working on the crime scene."

"But I wanted to stay in the annex," Amy interrupted.

"I'm afraid that's out of the question," Fred told her.

"I can come now," Abigail offered.

"You need to get your guest settled first," Fred countered. "I'll meet you in front of your room in an hour."

Abigail glanced at the clock and then gasped. "I had no idea it was so late."

Fred nodded. "I have a lot more to do before I can call it a night, too. I'll see you later." He turned and walked to the door.

"I'm starving," Amy told her as the door shut behind Fred.

"Our room rates include dinner and breakfast," Abigail replied. "I'll have to see if Marcia is still around, though. Dinner service usually stops at seven."

She picked up her cell and sent Marcia a quick message.

While she was waiting for a reply, she turned back to Amy. "I've put you in room 21M. It's on the second floor, here in the main building."

Amy sighed deeply. "I suppose that will have to do."

After awkwardly clearing her throat, Abigail told her the price. "That's per night, but, as I said, it includes dinner and breakfast."

"I don't see that I have much choice, do I? You're the only place to stay in Nightshade, and I need to be in Nightshade."

Abigail's cell buzzed, saving her from having to reply. She read the message on the screen and then smiled at Amy. "Marcia is still here, and she's happy to give us both some dinner."

"Great," Amy replied unenthusiastically. "I'll just put my case in my room first."

"I'll just need your credit card," Abigail told her. "How many nights are you planning on staying?"

Amy frowned. "I don't really know. At least two, I suppose, but maybe more." She dug into her purse and then pulled out a wallet. "I do hope none of my cards get canceled because of Russ's death. That doesn't happen, does it?"

"Do you have any just in your name?"

"Try this one," Amy said, handing her a card with Russ's name on it.

"I'd rather try one with your name on it. I really need the card to match your identification, which I'm going to need to see."

"Identification? Why?"

"It's standard practice in the hotel industry."

"I've never been asked for ID in a hotel before."

"I believe there are some lovely hotels in Corning."

Amy stared at her. "I'm a grieving widow. You can't seriously be threatening to throw me out just hours after my husband's body was found in your hotel. You should be falling all over yourself trying to keep me happy so that I don't sue you for inadequate security."

"I think it might be best if you found somewhere else to stay," Abigail said slowly, keeping her tone steady even as she felt her blood pressure rising. She'd worked in the industry for far too long to let a customer see how she was truly feeling.

"I want to stay here," Amy replied petulantly.

"Then I need to see identification, and I need a credit card in your name. I'll charge you for two nights for now, but you can extend your stay if you need to do so later."

For a moment, Abigail thought the woman was going to refuse. The two stared at one another for several seconds before Amy finally sighed and then looked back down at her wallet.

"Here's my license. It's a terrible picture."

Abigail carefully wrote down all of the information on the woman's license before using her phone to take a picture of it as well. When she handed it back, Amy gave her a credit card. It took the computer several minutes to process the card, but Abigail wasn't about to hand over any keys until she was certain the charge had gone through. Once she'd received an approval code, she opened the safe and found a key for the room she'd assigned to Amy.

"I'll show you to your room," she said, walking around the desk.

Amy looked at her and then down at her suitcase and back at her.

"Follow me," Abigail suggested, turning and walking away.

It took Amy a moment to pull up the handle on the case and follow. Abigail led her to the sweeping curved staircase just beyond the lobby.

"No elevator?" Amy demanded as Abigail started up the stairs.

"There's a service elevator in the kitchen. We can go that way if you'd prefer, but it's only a single flight of stairs."

After another loud sigh, Amy picked up her case and started up the stairs.

"Here we are," Abigail said a moment later, stopping in front of the door to 21M. She used the key to unlock the door and then pushed it open and stepped back to let Amy enter first. As Amy pushed past her, Abigail switched on the lights and then swallowed a happy sigh as she looked around the beautiful room.

As Jack and Janet had grown older, they'd spent less and less time and effort on maintaining the lodge. Some of the rooms on the third and fourth floor were badly in need of redecorating, but the rooms on the second floor had all received fresh coats of paint and new carpeting even while Jack and Janet had been searching for someone to buy the property. The bedroom furniture was solid and timeless, and the bathrooms had been redone no more than five or six years earlier. When Abigail and Mandy had come to view the property, they'd stayed in rooms on the second floor, and Abigail knew that those rooms were a large part of what they'd both loved about Sunset Lodge.

"It's adequate," Amy said with a sniff.

"Great. Do you want some time to freshen up before dinner?"

Amy glanced around the room and then shrugged. "I may as well go to dinner now. I'm both starving and far too sad to eat."

"You need to look after yourself, no matter what," Abigail replied almost automatically.

"Yes, I suppose so. Russ would want me to take care of myself. He loved me very much."

"Meals are served in the main dining room," Abigail said as they walked down the stairs. "There's a card in your room

67

that gives the mealtimes and menus, but because we aren't truly open for guests at the moment, we can be a bit more flexible, if you'd prefer to eat at a different time."

"What about the menu? Can I request something other than what's on the menu?"

"Marcia may be able to make some small changes, but you'll have to talk to her about that."

When they reached the ground floor, Abigail led Amy down the corridor to the dining room. Marcia walked in from the kitchen a moment later.

"Good evening," she said, smiling at Abigail.

Marcia was a motherly-looking woman with grey hair that was kept in a tidy bun at all times. When she was working in the kitchen, she always wore one of a dozen or more old-fashioned aprons. Tonight's was plain and dark grey.

Wondering if the apron was a nod to Amy's status as a widow in mourning, Abigail introduced Amy to Marcia.

"It's very nice to meet you," Marcia said. "When Carl told me that you'd arrived, I decided that I should stay late, in case you needed some dinner. I'm very sorry for your loss."

"Thank you," Amy said softly. "I'm not very hungry."

"But you need to eat," Marcia insisted. "You need to keep yourself healthy for the days and weeks ahead. I'll just fix plates for the both of you. I'll be right back."

"Plates of what?" Amy asked as Marcia rushed out of the room.

"It's Tuesday, so it should be chicken with rice and vegetables," Abigail told her.

"I suppose that will do," Amy replied. "I could really do with a glass of wine."

"We don't serve alcohol here. After dinner, I can give you directions to the nearest bar."

"I have vodka in my suitcase."

Abigail swallowed a dozen different questions. "Would you like a soft drink?" was what she finally asked.

"Sure, diet whatever."

There was a small refrigerator in the corner of the room so guests could help themselves to soft drinks, juice, and bottled water. Abigail poured drinks for Amy and herself and then put them on the table. Marcia was back a moment later with two plates full of food.

"Here we are. Give me a shout when you're ready for dessert," she said as she put the plates on the table.

"Have a seat," Abigail said

Amy dropped heavily into the chair next to her and picked up her fork. "I'll never eat all of this," she said before taking her first bite.

Abigail didn't bother to reply. As she began to eat, she realized that she was starving. The pair ate in silence for several minutes. Abigail was just swallowing her last bite of rice when Marcia returned.

"Very good," she said as she looked at the two empty plates on the table. "I have either chocolate cake or caramel cookie ice cream for dessert. Of course, you've both had a shock today. Maybe a bit of both?"

"Yes, please," Abigail said.

"Whatever," Amy replied.

Marcia took away the empty plates and returned a moment later with their desserts. As Abigail took a bite of cake, Amy spoke.

"What shock did you have today?" she asked.

"I, um, found the body," Abigail replied awkwardly.

There was a short silence before Amy replied.

"Did he look as if he'd suffered terribly?" she asked as a tear slid down her cheek.

"Not at all. I couldn't actually see much. I called the police after I opened the door and shouted, but the man on the bed didn't move," Abigail replied, trying to work out the right things to say.

Amy wiped her eyes with the back of her hand and then pushed her plate away. "I need to go and lie down. I'll probably drink some vodka and then sob myself to sleep. Good night."

Sighing, Abigail took a bite of ice cream and watched as the woman left the room.

"Is she okay?" Marcia asked as she rejoined Abigail.

"I've no idea."

"She didn't eat her dessert."

"No, but she did eat her dinner, at least. You should eat her dessert so it doesn't go to waste."

"I should, shouldn't I?" Marcia chuckled. She sat down where Amy had been sitting and picked up a fork. "I didn't have any cake after my dinner. I'm trying to cut down, actually, but it would be a shame to waste it."

"It's wonderful."

"Thank you. I don't know why I worry. Howard isn't going anywhere. He loves me even though I've put on a few pounds over the years."

"I've told Amy that we can be flexible about her meals. I hope that's okay."

"It's fine. She's just lost her husband. I'll do everything I can to accommodate her."

"Even though her husband conned you out of some money?"

"I hope she didn't know what sort of man she was married to, although she looked like a schemer. I wouldn't be surprised to learn that she is just as much of a con artist as her late husband."

"I hope you're wrong, but I did make her pay for her stay in advance."

Marcia laughed. "You've been in the business for long enough to recognize potential trouble."

"I hope so." She finished the last of her cake and pushed the empty plate away. "As always, thank you for a delicious meal."

"It's my pleasure. I'll see you at breakfast."

"Yes, and then we'll have our first proper staff meeting at one o'clock in the lobby."

"I'm looking forward to it. Carl said you were going to share all sorts of ideas for ways to build the business."

"Mandy and I have a long list of things we want to try, but it's all going to take time. A lot of the rooms need new paint and carpets before we can start renting them out."

"Howard and I are pretty good with brushes and rollers if you want a hand with the painting."

"Thank you. I may take you up on that." She glanced at the clock on the wall and sighed. "And now I have to go and pack my things so I can move into the main building. Fred is making the entire annex off limits."

"I can't say that I blame him."

"No, I suppose not."

Chapter Seven

"I'm sorry about this," Fred said as he lifted the police tape that was now surrounding the entire annex building.

Abigail ducked under it and then walked to the door to her room. "It's fine. I'd rather not stay out here right now anyway."

Fred nodded. "I understand your concerns, but I can assure you that Nightshade is a very safe community. This is the first murder case that I've ever been called upon to investigate in all my years here."

"It's still scary that someone was murdered just two doors away from where I was sleeping," she replied as she unlocked her door and pushed it open.

"Maybe you'll want to move into the main building for good."

"I just might." Abigail walked into the small room that had been her temporary home for the past two weeks. A pair of lamps on the bedside table came on when she flipped the switch near the door. They did their best to illuminate the room, but they still left large sections of the space in shad-

THE BODY IN THE ANNEX

ows. Sighing, she dug out her suitcase and began opening drawers.

"Why aren't you staying in the main building?" Fred asked. "That isn't an official police question. I'm just curious."

Abigail shrugged. "We have a lot of work to do just about everywhere. When we visited the property, Mandy and I agreed that the main building should be our first priority, but now that I'm here, I'm not certain where we should actually start." She sighed. "To be honest, I've been rather paralyzed with indecision, which isn't at all like me."

"Moving here was a big life change."

"It was, and it hasn't helped that all of our plans changed at the last minute. Anyway, since the rooms on the third and fourth floor of the main building need a lot of work and the rooms out here do too, I thought I should leave the four rooms on the second floor of the main building empty in case we suddenly got a few guests. This room isn't as bad as some of the others, but I still wouldn't put a guest in here."

"But 2A is in better condition?"

"2A was in better condition," Abigail said sadly. "Now I think I'll lock the door and never open it again."

She dropped the last of her clean T-shirts into the case and then walked into the adjoining bathroom. Fred followed and stood in the doorway of the tiny room as she filled a large plastic bag with all of her toiletries and makeup. Once she'd added the bag to her suitcase, she looked around the room.

"Got everything you need?" Fred asked.

"I should bring the bag of laundry, too," she said. "I may need those clothes if I can't get back in here for more than a few days."

"It's probably best if you take everything you could possibly need for a week or so."

"I'm leaving my winter clothes here. Let's hope it doesn't snow this week."

Fred laughed. "We do get a lot of snow, but not usually this early in the season. You should be okay for this week."

Abigail zipped her suitcase shut and then looked around the room again. She hadn't brought much out of the annex aside from clothes. The few boxes of personal possessions that she'd brought with her from New York City were tucked away in one of the fourth-floor rooms in the main building. She hadn't seen any point in making herself at home in the annex as staying there was only meant to be temporary.

"If I discover that I've forgotten something important, I can always call you and beg you to let me back in again, can't I?" she asked.

Fred frowned. "Of course you can," he said, clearly reluctantly.

"And now you need to get back to work. I'll get out of the way."

"Where are you going to stay while we're working in the annex?"

"Probably in one of the second-floor rooms. They're in the best condition, and I'm not interested in having any more guests right now."

"We may well be here all night and into tomorrow. Even after we leave, the police tape is going to remain in place. I don't know when we will be able to let you back into the annex."

Abigail ducked back under the police tape, dragging her suitcase and carrying her bag of laundry. When she looked back as she approached the main building, Fred was standing in front of her door, watching her progress. Since she didn't have a free hand, she didn't bother to wave after she'd wrestled open the door to the main building. She was kicking her laundry across the lobby when Carl walked into the room.

"Good evening," he said.

"Hi," she replied, blushing. She quickly picked up the bag.

"Where did you put our guest?" he asked as Abigail crossed the room.

"She's in 21M."

"And where are you going to stay tonight?"

"I thought I'd move into 22M for the time being."

Carl nodded slowly, a frown on his face. "I was thinking, I mean, I don't want to worry you, but I was thinking that it might be better if I stayed here tonight, too."

Abigail stared at him for a moment. "You want to stay in the main building, instead of in your cottage?"

"I don't think you should be alone in the building – not under the circumstances."

"I'm not alone. Amy Morris is here, too."

"That's one of the circumstances I was talking about."

"Are you suggesting that you think that Amy killed her husband?"

"No, not exactly. I'm just suggesting that you don't know anything about her. I don't think you should be too trusting, that's all."

"What do you think she's going to do?"

"Nothing, really," Carl replied with a sigh. "But it's always possible that she might be the killer's next target."

Abigail gasped. "You think the killer is going to strike again?"

"Maybe. I have no idea, really, but I have heard that killing people gets easier after the first one."

Shuddering, Abigail shook her head. "I'm sure I'll be fine here tonight. The front door will be locked, and I'll be behind a locked door in my room. Arnold will be down here, keeping an eye on things, too."

"Did I hear my name?" Arnold Nagel walked in from the back of the building, one hand idly scratching his bald head as he went.

"Good evening," Abigail said, smiling at the tall man whose T-shirt was molded to his muscular chest and arms.

"How are you?" he asked as he pulled Abigail into a hug. "Karen sent a hug, too," he added as he squeezed her again. "She's very upset about the murder, although I think she might be more upset that Rusty Morris was actually back in town than anything else."

"Did he con her out of a lot of money?" Abigail asked.

"Not Karen," Arnold replied. "She was far too smart to fall for what Rusty was doing. Unfortunately, her father wouldn't listen to her when she warned him about Rusty. He gave the man at least half of his savings – money that was supposed to see him through his retirement."

"That's terrible," Abigail said.

"Rusty was a horrible person, and I'm finding it difficult to be sorry that he's gone," Arnold told her.

"Well, don't let our guest hear you say that," Abigail replied. "You know the man's widow is staying here, don't you?"

Arnold nodded. "Carl filled us all in. Karen wants to come over and talk to the woman, but I told her I didn't think that was wise."

"I think you're right about that. We've no idea how much she knows about the things her husband did while he was living here, but that's a problem for the police, not us," Abigail replied. "She said they'd only been married for a year, so she probably has no idea why everyone in Nightshade hated her husband."

"Maybe someone ought to tell her, nicely, before she decides to go out for a meal or something and ends up being confronted by half a dozen angry strangers," Arnold suggested.

"That's a good point, actually," Abigail said with a sigh. "She really does need to know, doesn't she?"

"But who is going to tell her?" Carl asked.

Arnold looked at Abigail. "It might be better coming from you."

"It might be better coming from Fred," she countered. "Surely it's a police matter."

"He's already spoken to her, though, hasn't he? I'm sure he's awfully busy investigating Rusty's murder. I would suggest that talking to Amy is rather urgent, really," Arnold replied.

Abigail shook her head. "I'm too tired to worry about it tonight. Maybe things will be clearer in the morning."

"My offer is still good," Carl said. "I can stay in the building with you, if you'd like."

"I don't think that's necessary," Abigail said slowly. She shut her eyes and then squeezed them more tightly shut as the image of the dead man popped into her head. "Maybe just for tonight," she said quickly.

Carl nodded. "We can start with just tonight."

Abigail opened the safe and pulled out the box of keys. After thinking for a moment, she handed Carl the key to room 23M, which was next door to Amy and across the hall from the room she was planning on staying in herself.

"You know where we'll all be if you need us," she told Arnold. "Are you planning on sleeping in your cottage tonight, or do you want a room in here, too?"

"I can't stay in the annex?" he asked. "My room out there is about as far away from where the body was found as you can be."

"Unfortunately, the police aren't letting anyone stay in any of the annex rooms," Abigail replied. "You're more than welcome to sleep in a room here, though."

Arnold shook his head. "I can sleep in the office. That's what I used to do when the lodge was full anyway. The couch in there is actually very comfortable."

"Are you sure?" Abigail asked around a yawn.

"I'm sure," he replied. "If I can't sleep, I can always go home, but I'd hate having to hike back over here in the middle of the night if our guest needs anything."

"I can take care of anything our guest needs. I'll be sleeping right across the hall from her," Abigail said.

"I'm the night manager. Dealing with the guests during the night is my problem. You go and get a good night's sleep," he replied firmly.

"I'm too tired to argue," Abigail said. "I'll see you both in the morning."

She put the box of keys back in the safe and then picked up her laundry and her suitcase. Carl grabbed a bag by his feet that Abigail hadn't noticed before and then followed her to the stairs.

"Good night," Arnold called as the pair began to climb.

Carl waved and Abigail muttered a reply. A moment later, after opening the door to her room, she turned to Carl who was standing in front of his own door.

"Good night," she said.

"Let's hope it's a quiet one," he replied before opening his door and disappearing inside the room.

Abigail let herself into her room and switched on the lights. She was too tired to appreciate the beautiful antique furniture and the thick carpeting under her feet. Without bothering to unpack anything other than what she absolutely needed, she got ready for bed and crawled between the sheets.

"No nightmares," she muttered to herself as she switched off the lamp by the bed.

"Good morning," Abigail said brightly as she walked into the dining room the next morning.

"Hey," Arnold replied, looking at her over the cup of coffee he was nursing.

"Morning," Carl said with a nod.

"What can I get you this morning?" Marcia asked as she walked into the room. "I made pancake batter. It seemed like a good morning for pancakes with lots of maple syrup and butter. But if you'd prefer eggs or cereal or something else, just ask."

"Pancakes sound wonderful," Abigail said with a sigh. "I'm going to get fat living here," she added as she walked to the table on the far wall that held the coffee pot, among other things.

"You could do with putting on a few pounds," Marcia told her.

"Marcia's cooking makes us all fat," Arnold said, patting his stomach. "I never ate things like pancakes before I came to work here."

"You only had two," Carl said, putting his empty plate toward the center of the table. "I had six."

"Pancakes are good for your soul," Marcia said as she picked up the empty plate. "I'll go and get yours," she told Abigail. "And some bacon to go with them."

Abigail nodded and took another sip of the coffee she'd poured for herself. As the hot liquid began to work its magic, she put the cup down and filled a glass with orange juice. Then she carried both of her drinks to the table and sat down opposite Arnold.

"You look really tired," she said.

"The phone started ringing around midnight," he told her. "That's when some reporter in Buffalo got wind of the story and decided that he needed to cover it, too. It took me a long time to get rid of him, because he kept calling back every time I tried hanging up on him."

"You should have just put the phone on silent and gone to bed," Abigail replied.

"I thought about it, but I was afraid our guest might wake up and need something. You're paying me to be available to guests at all hours."

"Did the man finally give up?" Carl asked.

"He did, but then someone from some news website in Rochester started calling." Arnold sighed. "There were others after that, but I stopped paying attention to where they were calling from. I just kept saying 'no comment' to everyone until they finally gave up."

"Did you manage to get any sleep?" Abigail asked.

"Some, in between calls, but not much. Now that you're here, I'm going to go and sleep until it's time for our meeting later. I'll see you all around one o'clock." Arnold got to his feet and then stretched and yawned.

"You don't have to come to the meeting," Abigail said quickly. "If you can sleep, stay in bed."

"If I stay in bed for too long, I'll mess up my whole system," he replied. "I'll be here at one."

He was gone before Abigail could protest any further. A moment later, her cell buzzed.

Just transferred the main number back to the phone behind the reception desk. Good luck.

She read the text and then sighed. Marcia bustled in a moment later, carrying a plate full of food.

"Here you are," she said. "Anything else?"

"This looks wonderful. Thank you. I need to go and get the phone, though. Apparently, people were calling all night, trying to find out more about the murder," Abigail said. She started to stand up, but Carl held up a hand.

"You stay and enjoy your breakfast," he said. "I'll go and sit behind the reception desk until you're done. I can answer the phone and play dumb. I'm very good at it."

Marcia and Abigail both laughed as the man slowly made his way out of the room.

"How are you today?" Abigail asked Marcia.

She shrugged. "I'll be better when whoever killed Rusty Morris is behind bars, but otherwise, I'm fine."

"I think we all feel that way."

"I know I do," Amy announced from the doorway.

"I hope you slept well," Abigail told her.

"I cried myself into an exhausted state, but I don't feel as if I slept at all. I have half an inch of concealer under each eye to try to hide my dark circles," she replied.

"It's doing a good job," Marcia said. "You don't look tired at all."

Abigail hid a smile behind her coffee mug. She'd been thinking much the same thing, but she hadn't wanted to say it.

"I just hope coffee will help," Amy said, crossing to the table and pouring herself a drink. She added three scoops of sugar and a generous dollop of cream to the cup and then gave it a quick stir. "That's better," she said after her first sip.

"We have pancakes for breakfast today," Marcia said. "Or I can make you some eggs, any style. Our breakfast meat is bacon."

Amy shook her head. "Oh, I can't possibly eat anything. I'm too exhausted and miserable to eat."

"You should have something," Abigail told her. "At least a cup of yogurt or some cereal."

Amy sighed dramatically. "I'm sure I can't manage a single bite, but if you want to bring me a few pancakes with maple syrup, I'll try to nibble on them."

Marcia smiled and nodded. "I won't be a minute," she said before she left the room.

"What are your plans for today?" Abigail asked as Amy took the seat next to her.

"I have no idea what I'm going to do with myself, today or

tomorrow or any day in the future, really. My entire world crashed down around me yesterday."

"Did Rusty talk about Nightshade with you much?" Abigail asked, trying to decide how much she wanted to tell the other woman about the man's past.

"Not at all, not until last week, when he suddenly announced that he was going to be away for a few days."

"So you don't know about the things that happened here ten years ago."

"What happened here ten years ago?" Amy asked.

Abigail took a deep breath. "I didn't live here then, but I've been told that Rusty came into town and expressed an interest in buying the Xanzibar Hotel."

"Oh, yes, he told me all about his plans for the Xanzibar. It was going to be amazing. I suppose you should be happy he never managed to get the hotel reopened. No one would want to stay at Sunset Lodge if they could stay at the Xanzibar."

Abigail opened her mouth to reply, but she stopped as the door swung open, and Carl walked in. Fred was right behind him.

"The phone's been ringing a lot," Carl said. "And now Fred needs to talk to you."

Abigail swallowed the last of her pancakes. "Right now?" she asked.

"Right now," Fred replied flatly.

"It sounds as if you're in trouble," Amy said.

"I'm sure that can't be the case," Abigail replied, trying to keep her tone light. Fred's frowning face was worrying, though. "We can talk more later," she said to Amy as she got up and followed Fred and Carl out of the room.

"I'll stay at reception," Carl said as they walked back toward the front of the building.

"We need to talk privately," Fred told Abigail.

"We can talk in my room," she offered.

He nodded. "I'll just get a female trooper to sit with us."

A few minutes later, Abigail unlocked the door to her room and then walked inside. Fred followed, with the uniformed female trooper on his heels. Abigail sat on the edge of the bed and tried to smile. "What can I do for you?" she asked.

Fred sat in a chair by the desk. The trooper stood near the door, staring straight ahead, her expression neutral.

"You can start by explaining to me why you never bothered to mention your connection to the dead man," Fred replied as he opened his notebook.

"My connection to the dead man?" Abigail echoed. "I'm not sure what you mean."

"I mean, you didn't bother to tell me that your sister dated Russell Morris for several months a few years ago."

Chapter Eight

Abigail stared, open-mouthed, at the police detective. "Mandy?"

"Do you have any other sisters?" he shot back.

"No, but I always wanted an older brother." She shook her head. "I'm sorry. I'm in shock and I'm babbling. Are you seriously telling me that my sister used to date Rusty Morris?"

"Are you trying to tell me that you didn't know? As I understand it, they dated for several months. I find it difficult to believe that she never talked about the man, even if she didn't introduce you to him."

"I find it difficult to believe, too. We're very close. We always talk about the men in our lives together. I don't know what to tell you, really."

Fred frowned. "You didn't know."

"I didn't know. If you can give me some dates, maybe I can try to remember something."

Fred looked down at this notebook and then slowly flipped back through the pages. "From what I was told, they started seeing one another almost exactly two years ago and they dated for around four months."

"So September through December? Two years ago? Were they still together at Christmas?"

"I'm not certain of that."

Abigail sat back and shut her eyes. "That was a really busy time for me at work. A well-known food critic gave us a glowing write-up in his paper sometime in August, and the restaurant was suddenly in huge demand. Then the hotel guests started complaining that they couldn't get a table or room service because the restaurant was too busy, so we started reserving a certain number of tables each night for hotel guests only. Then we started selling out of hotel rooms."

"I'm not sure why that matters," Fred said flatly.

"It matters because I don't think I saw Mandy more than once or twice a month during that period. We talked on the phone every other day or so, but I usually called her when I got home from work, and we never talked for long because we were both tired by that time of night. I vaguely remember her saying something about seeing someone new, but I don't remember her ever mentioning his name. She may have, I suppose, but if she did, it simply didn't register."

"So in your opinion, the relationship wasn't anything serious?"

"She never said anything to me to suggest that the relationship was anything serious. I missed Thanksgiving with our parents that year, but I was there for Christmas. She didn't bring him to Christmas dinner, which I would have expected her to do if it was serious."

"Maybe they split up before Christmas."

"She didn't take him to Thanksgiving dinner, either. I would have heard all about it if she had."

"Interesting," Fred said, making a note.

"I wish I could tell you more. Obviously, I'm going to call Mandy as soon as you leave. I assume she's already been questioned."

"She has, yes, or rather she's being questioned right now."

"I'm sorry that you thought that I'd withheld information from you."

Fred nodded and then got to his feet. "We'll be working in the annex all day today. I'll be there if you remember anything interesting."

Abigail watched as the man walked out of the room. He still seemed to think that she'd deliberately withheld information from him. Sighing, she crossed to the reception desk.

"I can take things from here," she told Carl. "You go and get started on all the other jobs on your list."

He nodded. "I'll see you at one," he said.

"Great."

With her mind racing in a million directions, she sent a *CALL ME* text to Mandy and then sat down behind the desk.

"You've been wandering around without direction for two weeks now. It's time to start taking this business seriously," she said sternly as she fired up the old computer. When her phone rang two hours later, she'd nearly finished making her long list of jobs that needed to be done before the lodge could open properly.

"Hello, Little Sis," she said into the device.

"I never made the connection," Mandy replied. "You said Mr. Morris when you told me about your dead guest. I never imagined that your Mr. Morris was Russell Morris, the man I'd dated."

"I hope you told the police that."

"Of course I did. I also told them that I never introduced you to Russell. Our relationship wasn't anything serious. I probably never even told you his name while we were dating."

"You may have, but if you did, I didn't remember it."

Mandy sighed. "We dated for a few months during that crazy busy period you had when that food critic said your restaurant had well-prepared food at prices that were actually reasonable."

Abigail laughed. "It wasn't exactly the most amazing review ever, but New Yorkers are always looking for a bargain."

"And then you were slammed with customers in the restaurant and guests in the hotel."

"We were, and that rush of extra customers gave the owners a chance to sell the business at a much higher price than they would have gotten otherwise, which led to the new owners that made my life miserable, which led me to here, which isn't working out at all the way I'd hoped."

"Do you want me to quit here and come and help?"

"Don't be silly. You can come and help once your job finishes, unless you line up another one right away."

"About that, um, I may have another job lined up."

"That's great. Broadway?"

Mandy laughed. "Not quite, but nearly. It's another off-Broadway production, but they want me to do all of the set design. It's an amazing opportunity to be involved in a great show."

"Congratulations. I'm really happy for you."

"But that means it will be at least a few more months before I can come and help with the business."

"You'll just have to help out more financially."

"I will. I promise."

The pair talked about money for a short while before Abigail sighed.

"But we were talking about Rusty Morris. Tell me everything."

"There truly isn't much to tell. I met him in a bar one night after a show. He was with some woman who was being rude and demanding to the staff. I was there with some of the other stage crew folks. He was clearly embarrassed by his date's behavior, and eventually he told her that he didn't think things were going well and that he was going to leave. She got mad and dumped her drink over his head. The rest of the bar applauded as she stormed out of the room. One of the guys in my group insisted on buying Russell a drink after everything he'd been through."

"And he agreed, even though he was dripping wet?"

Mandy laughed. "The glass was mostly ice, actually. It bounced off his head and all over the floor, but it wasn't too bad."

"So then what happened?"

"He sat down next to me, and we started talking about how hard it is to meet people in New York. His date had been a blind date that a friend of his had arranged, and he swore it was his last blind date ever. It was just a casual conversation, but when the evening ended, he asked for my number."

"And you gave it to him."

"He was attractive, smart, and funny. Why shouldn't I have given it to him?"

"And then you dated for four months?"

"Was it that long? I suppose it might have been. I was pretty busy with a show, but he called a few days later, and we had dinner together a few nights after that. We had brunch together a few days later, and then he had to go somewhere for work, and we didn't see one another for a few weeks. He called a few times while he was away, but mostly just to say hello."

"And you never mentioned him to me."

"I would have if it had turned into anything serious. We had dinner together a few more times after he got back, but it never went much beyond that. He hinted more than once that we should sleep together, but I didn't feel as if we were at that stage in the relationship yet. He didn't argue, but he also didn't make any effort to see me more often or to try to get more serious. He was traveling for work a lot, and then I started a new show, which meant working a lot more hours, and we sort of just drifted along until just before Christmas when he simply stopped calling."

"He stopped calling? Were you terribly upset?"

"Not terribly. It was one of those relationships that never really got off the ground. I sort of felt that if either of us had made a bit more effort, it might have really turned into something, but for whatever reason, neither of us ever did."

"When did you see him last?"

"The police asked me that, too. It was in early December. We had dinner together the week after Thanksgiving. I hadn't invited him to come back to Pennsylvania with me for the holiday, and he hadn't invited me to join him wherever he went, so things felt a bit awkward at that dinner. He called me a few times after that, and we even made plans once or twice, but none of them ever actually came to fruition."

"Because he canceled, or you did?"

"I think I canceled once, and he canceled the other time. I don't really remember, though. It wasn't important at the time."

"It might be important now."

"Why? I mean, even if he broke my heart and left me desperate for revenge, I didn't have anything to do with his murder. I was here, with half a dozen other people, the night Rusty died."

"You may have been there, but I was here," Abigail said flatly.

There was a long silence on the other end. "Surely the police don't think that you would kill a man because he'd dumped me two years ago."

"I don't know what they think, but it's possible. The

detective in charge of the investigation was very angry that I didn't tell him you'd dated the dead man."

"You didn't know."

"I know I didn't know, but I can't prove that I didn't know. Even if I had known, it seems a weak motive when compared to everyone else, anyway."

"Oh? There are people there with motives?"

Abigail sighed. "I forgot I haven't spoken to you since I found the body. Apparently, Rusty was in Nightshade once before. While he was here, he managed to persuade just about everyone in town to invest in his business. He claimed he was going to be reopening the hotel at the other end of the lake."

"I saw that when we were there. It's huge, and it looks as if it's been abandoned for decades."

"It has been, but Rusty told everyone he was going to buy it and restore it. From what I've heard, nearly everyone in town gave him at least some money toward the plan."

"What happened?" Mandy demanded.

"Rusty disappeared one night, right after a big charity fundraiser for the project. The local paper suggested that he got away with half a million dollars."

"If only," a voice said behind Abigail.

She spun around. "I didn't know you were there," she told Amy.

"If you had, you would have been nicer about Russ, wouldn't you?" Amy replied. "But I know all about what the people in Nightshade thought of him. He came back to show them that he'd been conned as much as they had, but he never had the chance."

"Do you need to go?" Mandy asked in Abigail's ear.

"Um, yes, actually. I think I do," Abigail replied. "I'll call you later today or maybe tomorrow."

"Love you, Big Sis."

"Love you, too."

Abigail pushed the button to end the call and then looked back at Amy. "He was conned, too?" she repeated.

Amy nodded. "He told me all about everything that happened when he was here. Even though it happened ten years or so ago, he was still upset about the entire situation. He'd worked really hard to raise money for the project and then, right when he thought it was all coming together, he had the rug ripped out from underneath his feet."

"I hope you told the police all of this."

"I did, of course, because whoever cheated Russ out of that money was probably also the person who killed him."

"What exactly happened?"

"Russ had been here for several weeks, getting investments. Then he had a big fundraising event that raised even more money. He was over the moon. He went to New York to sign the final papers for the purchase of the property, but when he handed over the check for the deposit, it bounced. Someone had cleared out the company's bank account. Russ was beside himself, but there wasn't anything he could do."

"Surely he should have called the police."

Amy nodded. "He should have. That was his second mistake, of course. He thought he knew who had taken the money, and at first he thought there had just been some miscommunication or something. Russ didn't want to get anyone into trouble, so he decided to find a way to fix everything without involving the police."

"He should have come back to Nightshade and explained everything to the people here."

"Yes, of course, but he didn't want to come back and tell them that he wasn't buying the Xanzibar after all. He didn't want to disappoint people."

"So he simply didn't come back at all."

"He did, though, and then someone murdered him before he could make everything right."

"Are you saying he'd tracked down the money and was now going to purchase the Xanzibar?"

Amy shrugged. "I don't know anything for sure. He just told me that he was going to Nightshade to sort out some things."

"What about his child?" Abigail asked.

"His what?"

"Someone told me that when he left, he left behind a pregnant girlfriend."

"He would never have done that," Amy protested. "I mean, he never would have gotten someone pregnant. Russ didn't want children."

"Not wanting them doesn't necessarily mean that he didn't get someone pregnant."

Amy shook her head. "He would have told me," she said. "The baby probably wasn't his. Yeah, that's it. Whoever the woman was, she probably lied about the baby being his after he'd already left town and couldn't defend himself."

Abigail didn't argue. Everything she'd heard from Jessica was second-hand information. Maybe Amy was right about the baby.

"And now I'm going to take a walk around the lake," Amy announced. "Russ told me that there's a nice paved path all the way around it. I want to walk in his footsteps. I want to see the Xanzibar, too. He had such high hopes for that place. I need to see it for myself."

"There is a path all the way around the lake, but some parts of the path are quite overgrown. Be careful."

Amy looked down at her expensive-looking heels. "Maybe I should change my shoes," she said softly before turning and heading for the stairs.

Abigail went back to work on her list. Amy walked past her a short while later, this time wearing sneakers. She waved to Abigail but didn't speak. By noon, Abigail's stomach was rumbling too much for her to concentrate. She printed out what she had and then went into the kitchen and threw together a snack. By the time she'd finished eating and cleaning up the kitchen, it was time for the staff meeting.

Carl and Arnold were both in the sitting area when Abigail walked back into the lobby. Abigail sat down across from them. Marcia rushed in a moment later.

"Good afternoon," Abigail said. "Thank you all for coming." She took a deep breath and then sighed. "All of that already sounded more formal than I want this to be. I've worked in both big and small hotels, but this is by far the smallest property I've ever managed. I'm really hoping that we can all work together as a team. I want you all to come to me with ideas for improvements we can make or with any concerns or issues you may have about anything. And I do mean anything. If you decide you aren't being paid enough or you need more vacation days or you get a much better offer from somewhere else, please come and talk to me."

"I can't see any of us leaving," Carl said. "We all love Sunset Lodge. When Jack and Janet first started talking about selling it, we thought about pooling our resources and buying it ourselves."

"Should I ask why you didn't do that?" Abigail wondered.

The trio exchanged glances. "There were a lot of problems with the idea," Carl said after an awkward minute. "Mostly, though, I think we all realized that we were happier just working here and not having to be responsible for the entire property."

Abigail nodded. "It's a huge responsibility, but Mandy and I are excited about the possibilities. It's taken me a few weeks to start feeling settled, but now it's time for all of us to get to work. I've started making lists of the jobs that need to be done and the order in which they need to be tackled. We're going to start by painting and freshening up the ground floor.

I'd like to replace some of the carpeting too, but I'm not sure we can afford that right now."

"There are about a dozen cans of paint in the basement," Carl told her. "Jack and Janet used the same color everywhere."

Abigail glanced at the beige walls and sighed. "I think I'd like to try using different colors in some of the rooms – nothing too dramatic, but something more interesting than this off-white shade."

"It's called 'Near Miss Gray,'" Carl replied. "Jack and Janet loved it."

"If the cans in the basement are still good, we may stick with it for a while," Abigail told him. "Using it up will be cheaper than buying anything else for now."

"I'll start bringing up the cans," Carl offered. "I can check each one and then put the good ones in one of the empty rooms on the third floor."

Abigail nodded. "That sounds like a great idea. Bring up any brushes and rollers, too. I'd like to get started in the lobby and the dining room as soon as possible."

Carl nodded and then made a note in the small notebook he carried. As he put the notebook back in his pocket, the hotel's front door slowly opened.

"Good afternoon," Abigail said to the woman who walked slowly into the room. She looked to be somewhere around forty, with light brown hair that was lightly streaked with gray. Her jeans and T-shirt looked clean and comfortable.

"Hi," she replied softly, giving Abigail a tentative smile.

"How can we help you?" Abigail asked after a moment.

The woman shrugged. "I don't really think you can. I just wanted to, I don't know, be here for some reason. It's hit me really hard, Rusty's death, and I wanted to, I don't know, pay my respects in some odd way."

"After the way you were treated, Rusty doesn't deserve your respects," Marcia said.

"I suppose not, but here I am," the woman replied.

"I'm Abigail Clark." She stood up and took a step toward the new arrival.

"Oh, hello. I'm Lisa Carter."

Chapter Nine

"I'm sorry for your loss," Abigail said, wondering if the words were appropriate under the circumstances.

"Thank you," Lisa replied, blushing. "Of course, I lost Rusty a long time ago, but this has still been incredibly hard. I suppose I'd never given up hope that he'd come back one day. I've moved on, of course, but I did rather hope that he'd decide to play a part in his son's life."

"How is Huey dealing with everything?" Marcia asked.

"He's upset and confused and angry and probably a dozen other emotions," Lisa replied. "Telling him was the hardest thing I've ever had to do, and the worst part is that I can't answer any of his questions. I don't know why Rusty was here. I don't know why Rusty was murdered. I don't know who killed him." Tears began to slide down the woman's cheeks.

Abigail walked to the desk and grabbed the tissue box. She handed it to Lisa, who gave her a grateful watery smile.

"Rusty didn't call you and tell you he was in town?" Carl asked.

Lisa shook her head. "If he had, I would have refused to see him, which is horrible, all things considered. Now I'll spend forever wishing I'd had just one more chance to see him again. More than anything, I wish I'd had a chance to introduce him to his son. I can't help but think that he'd have been proud of Huey."

"He's a good kid," Arnold said. "I enjoy working with him on the track."

"He loves running, and we're grateful to you for helping coach the track team for the schools," Lisa replied.

"I'm happy to do it. I'd coach the weightlifting team if they had one, but since they don't, I'm happy to work with the track and field teams at every level."

Lisa looked around the room. "I haven't been in here in years, not since Rusty left, I suppose. It looks the same, though."

"I'm hoping to do some modernizing, but I don't really want to change much," Abigail told her.

"I hope you don't. Sunset Lodge is part of the town's history, and it shouldn't ever change," Lisa replied.

Abigail didn't argue. If the woman visited only once every ten years, Abigail wasn't about to take her opinions into account when it came to what she wanted to do with the property.

"Come and sit down," Marcia suggested, patting the couch next to her. "When did you find out about Rusty?" she asked as Lisa settled on the seat.

"Fred came and told me last night. I was surprised that he'd managed to keep it quiet up until then, really. I'd heard that something had happened up at the lodge, but I didn't even know that someone had been murdered until Fred appeared at my door."

"Ross must be furious that he missed the story," Carl said with a chuckle.

"It's all over the paper's website today, of course," Lisa replied. "But it wasn't there when I went to bed last night.

There was just a small article about how the police had been called to Sunset Lodge."

"I can't believe Ross didn't drive up here himself to see what was happening," Marcia said.

"Yesterday was the groundbreaking for the new furniture store outside of town," Lisa told her. "Ross was there with a bunch of reporters from Buffalo and Rochester. It's the first store in the very popular chain to open in New York, and everyone is talking about it."

"But it's going to be about half an hour away, isn't it?" Carl asked.

Lisa nodded. "But it's even farther from Buffalo and Rochester, and those papers covered it."

"And Ross missed the biggest Nightshade news story of the decade," Arnold laughed.

"I'm surprised he hasn't been calling every half hour," Lisa told Abigail.

"I'm letting the machine take calls right now," she replied. "He may well be calling."

Lisa shrugged. "He was at my door this morning, demanding a statement. I told him to shove his statement up his, um, well, I told him that I didn't want to comment."

"I don't blame you. What could you possibly say?" Marcia asked, patting the woman's arm.

"Huey is always my first concern. There was no way I was going to say anything bad about Rusty to Ross. Rusty was Huey's father, whether I like it or not."

"Was he, though?" a voice asked from the doorway.

Marcia gasped, and Lisa looked shocked as Amy strolled into the lobby.

"Bad timing?" she asked with a nasty smirk.

"Ah, Lisa, this is Amy Morris," Abigail said. "Amy is Rusty's widow."

Lisa raised an eyebrow. "I'm sorry for your loss," she said blandly.

"Russ told me about you," Amy replied. "About how after he left Nightshade you sent him a letter, telling him that you were pregnant with his child. Of course, he barely knew who you were, but that didn't stop you from trying to get money from him."

"My dear, I'm sorry to tell you this, but Rusty lied to you," Marcia said. "Lisa and Rusty were very much a couple for the months while he was living here. Everyone in town knew they were together, and when we found out that Lisa was pregnant, we all knew who the father had to be."

Amy shrugged. "They may have dated for a few weeks, but it wasn't anything serious. The baby wasn't his."

"Of course the baby was his," Marcia snapped.

Lisa held up a hand. "I can't see that it matters," she said sadly. "Rusty isn't here and will never be able to play a part in his son's life. I never asked the man for a penny while he was alive, and I don't expect to get anything from him now that he's gone. You may believe whatever you like. It truly doesn't matter," she told Amy.

"Can I get that in writing?" Amy demanded.

"Get what in writing?" Lisa asked.

"That you don't want anything from Russ's estate, of course," Amy replied.

"She's worried that you're going to sue on behalf of Huey," Arnold said. "And you really should. Huey should be entitled to inherit something from his father."

"Russ wasn't his father," Amy nearly shouted.

"I'm not going to sue you," Lisa told her. "But I'm also not going to sign anything. I can't help but hope that Rusty might have left something to Huey in his will. He probably didn't, but he might have."

"He didn't," Amy said sharply. "We rewrote our wills when we got married. He left everything he had to me."

"I hope you and Rusty's stolen money are very happy together, then," Lisa replied. "I should be going."

"He never stole any money," Amy said. "It all got a lot more complicated than he'd expected it to, but he was working it out. He was in town to announce his new plans."

"New plans? I think he'd have struggled to find anyone interested in listening to his new plans," Carl said.

Amy sighed. "You all want to think the worst of him."

"We all lost money to him," Marcia countered. "He got nearly everyone in Nightshade to invest in his scheme, and then he disappeared with all of the money. And he left Lisa behind, all alone and pregnant. It's difficult not to think the worst of him."

"I've said all I'm going to say about the baby that wasn't his," Amy replied. "As for the money, he was here to sort all of that out."

"How?" Carl demanded.

Amy shrugged. "I'm not sure. He didn't share all of his plans with me. He just said that he was going to make everything right in Nightshade."

"I don't believe it," Carl told her. "He came here to try to swindle us all out of even more money."

"I don't have to stand here and listen to this. I know the truth about the man that I loved. He felt terrible about everything that happened in Nightshade – well, not the baby, of course, because that wasn't his, but he felt terrible about the money. He knew that everyone here blamed him when everything went wrong, but it wasn't his fault." She sighed. "I never should have come."

"That makes two of us," Lisa said, getting to her feet.

"It was nice meeting you," Abigail said.

Lisa nodded. "Everyone in town was happy to hear that

someone had bought Sunset Lodge. We were worried that Jack and Janet might decide to retire and leave it empty if they couldn't find a buyer before too much longer. The last thing we need is another empty property on the lake."

"Knock, knock," a voice said as the door swung open. The man who walked into the room looked around and then blushed. He was an attractive man who looked to be around forty, and he was wearing jeans and a sweatshirt that advertised a college football team. "Hi," he said awkwardly.

"Ken? What are you doing here?" Lisa demanded.

He shrugged. "The longer I sat at home waiting for you to get back, the more worried I got. You know I didn't think you should come up here."

Lisa nodded. "And you know that I needed to come up here to – I don't know – get some closure or something."

"And has it helped?" he asked.

"Not really," Lisa replied with a sigh.

"Hello," Amy said softly. She took a step closer to Ken and smiled brightly at him. "I'm Amy Jackson. It's very nice to meet you."

"Ken Carter," the man replied, taking a step backward as Amy moved closer.

"My husband," Lisa added as she walked toward Ken.

"Huey's father," Amy suggested.

"I'm Huey's step-father," Ken told her. "Sadly, Huey's biological father didn't want to be a part of his life, but I was more than happy to step in and raise Huey as my own."

"So you won't be expecting Huey to inherit anything," Amy suggested.

Ken frowned. "Inherit anything? From his father, you mean? I hadn't really thought about it, but I suppose not. As far as I know, Rusty Morris never actually acknowledged Huey as his son."

"Because he wasn't," Amy replied.

"Amy is Rusty's widow," Lisa interjected before Ken could reply. "She's very worried that we might sue her or Rusty's estate on Huey's behalf."

"Can we do that?" Ken asked.

"No!" Amy snapped.

"Of course we can," Lisa said. "We can talk about it later, at home."

Ken looked from Lisa to Amy and back again. "We're doing a good job bringing up Huey without any help from his father," he said. "I reckon we can keep doing what we're doing without any help from his father's estate."

Lisa nodded. "I do think that it would be nice if Huey had something from his father, though. I've saved everything that Rusty ever gave me, but it isn't much."

"If you want Huey to have something from his father, maybe you should work out who his father actually was," Amy suggested.

Lisa inhaled slowly. "All you're doing is making me want to sue," she told the other woman. "I'm more than happy to get a DNA test to prove that Rusty was Huey's father."

"Russ never lied to me," Amy said.

But you don't look completely convinced, Abigail thought.

"We should go," Lisa told Ken.

"I still don't understand why you wanted to come here," he said.

"I'm not sure I understand why I wanted to come here," Lisa replied. "But I do know why I want to leave." She glanced at Amy and then turned and walked out of the room. Ken rushed to follow her.

"That poor man," Amy said as she turned and walked toward the stairs. "His wife has been lying to him for so many years."

"I'm afraid you're the one who has been lied to," Marcia told her. "Huey is Rusty's child. If I were you, I'd start thinking about giving Lisa and Ken a fair portion of Rusty's estate."

Amy stopped and stared at her for a moment. "Thank you for your unwanted opinion. They aren't entitled to anything, but even if they were, I shall be honoring what Rusty put in his will, not what some random stranger thinks I ought to do."

She stomped out of the room before anyone else could speak.

"That was interesting," Arnold said. "If I were Lisa, I'd get a DNA test done fast before the body is shipped to wherever Amy wants to take it."

"That's a good point," Marcia said. "I think I'll call Lisa and suggest that." She pulled out her phone and tapped the screen a few times. "Just setting a reminder," she told Abigail. "I'll take care of it later."

Abigail nodded. "But where were we?" she asked. "We were talking about all of the things that I want to do, starting with painting every room on this floor."

"The rooms on the second floor aren't too bad," Carl said. "I painted all of them a few years ago, and they had new carpeting not long ago as well."

"So once we get the lobby and the dining room painted, we'll touch up the paintwork on the second floor as needed. Then I want to reopen with just those four rooms available," Abigail told them. "If I can generate a bit of income while we're working on the rest of the place, that will help. I think it makes sense to focus on this building for now. We'll work though the rooms on the third floor next and then the fourth."

"What about the annex?" Arnold asked when Abigail fell silent.

"I'm not sure what I want to do with the annex," she replied with a sigh. "Mostly, I'm not sure what to do with

2A. I can't imagine ever having a guest stay in that room again. I'm not sure I ever want to go back in that room, actually."

"We can use it for storage while we're working on the other rooms," Arnold suggested.

Abigail nodded. "Carl and I discussed that earlier. It certainly makes sense to do that while we're working on the annex. We can move the furniture from each room in turn into there, which will make painting and decorating a lot easier."

"I'm glad I'll be too busy in the kitchen to help," Marcia said. "I don't want to go anywhere near the annex."

"What about the cottages?" Arnold asked.

"Unless something happens to change my mind, they're going to be the last thing I tackle after the main house and the annex are both done," Abigail replied. "Mandy was supposed to be coming up with a theme for each cottage before we started redecorating them. She's too busy to do that right now, but I'd rather not paint and put down new carpeting in the cottages before she's had a chance to decide what fits each theme she wants to create."

"The cottages make a lot of money in the summer," Arnold said.

"Summer seems a long way off," Abigail replied. "We have a lot of work to do in here and in the annex before summer."

"Is that the goal? To have the main house and the annex ready for summer?" Carl asked.

"Obviously, the sooner the better, but I'm trying to be realistic with my expectations. I want to do as much of the work as I can myself, but that means it's going to take a lot longer than it would if I hired a crew to come in and paint and decorate."

"I can do a lot of the painting," Carl said. "In between my other jobs."

"I'm happy to do some painting, too," Marcia told her. "I have time between breakfast and dinner every day."

"And I can give you a few hours every afternoon," Arnold added.

"I appreciate the offers," Abigail began.

Marcia held up a hand. "Don't say anything else," she said. "We want to help, and you don't have to pay us extra for a bit of our extra time. There was a time, not long ago, when we all thought we were going to be out of work and homeless. If you and Mandy hadn't bought the lodge when you did, that may well have happened. We're all happy to do whatever we can to help you make the business a success again."

Abigail thought about arguing, but she really couldn't afford to pay them extra if they helped with the painting, not unless they started getting guests on a regular basis, which seemed unlikely with the fall and winter months ahead. "Thank you," she said after a moment.

"Should we start today?" Arnold asked, looking eager.

"Carl needs to dig out the paint so we can see what we have," Abigail replied. "I think I'd like to wait to start until after the police have gone as well. Let's plan to start painting on Monday. If the police are still here at that point, we'll just ignore them."

"That sounds like a plan," Carl said.

Abigail looked down at her notes. "Once we get the business back up and running, Mandy and I have all sorts of ideas for ways to bring in guests. Mandy made a long list of themed weekends we could try, from seventies discos, to eighties nights, to murder mysteries, to themes around television shows."

"That all sounds fun," Marcia said. "Maybe I could do different food for each different weekend."

"That would be part of it," Abigail told her. "You wouldn't mind?"

"Mind?" Marcia echoed. "I've been making the same meals every week for the past twenty-odd years. Jack and Janet liked to keep things exactly the same so that guests always knew what to expect. I'd be delighted to make something different once in a while. If you give me some ideas about the different themes, I can start looking up recipes now."

Abigail grinned at the woman's obvious excitement. "I was afraid the idea might upset you."

"Not at all," Marcia assured her.

Looking back down at her list, Abigail frowned. "I think that's about all I wanted to go over today, aside from encouraging all of you to come to talk to me at any time. If you have any suggestions for themes for weekends or any other ideas of ways to bring in some extra income, please let me know."

"I'll think about it," Arnold said as he got to his feet. "For now, though, I think I'm going to take a nap." He was yawning as he left the room.

"I'm going to go and get started finding paint cans," Carl said. "The sooner we can get started on the painting, the sooner we can start having guests again." He rushed away as Abigail and Marcia stood up together.

"I'm going to go and start searching the internet for recipes from the seventies and the eighties," Marcia said. "Unless you have any other ideas?"

"It's a place to start, anyway," Abigail replied. "Feel free to change up the daily menu whenever you want so that you can test what you find. When we have guests, we'll need to tell them what's going to be available each night, but when it's just us, cook whatever you want."

"Really? How exciting! I haven't cooked whatever I wanted in such a long time. I hope I haven't forgotten how to cook properly." She was still chatting excitedly to herself as she walked out of the room.

Abigail walked back to the reception desk and frowned at

the answering machine. The message light was blinking frantically. She was still busy deleting messages from various reporters when the lodge's front door opened.

"Hi," the attractive blond man said as he walked into the room. "I hope I'm not bothering you. I'm Tom Evans. I wanted to talk to you about remodeling the lodge."

Chapter Ten

"Hi," Abigail replied before introducing herself.

"It's a real pleasure to meet you," Tom said. He looked around the lobby and smiled. "This is a beautiful old building. One I've been dying to get my hands on for years."

"Oh?"

He shrugged. "I'm a general contractor, working on both new construction and remodeling and updating of older properties. My passion is updating really old buildings like this lodge. Jack and Janet were happy with it just the way it is, but it has so much potential. I'm sure you'd love to make some improvements."

Abigail nodded. "We're already getting started by giving all of the rooms on the ground floor a fresh coat of paint."

Tom sighed. "Paint? I mean, I suppose I can't argue that the walls need painting, but wouldn't it be wonderful to do more than just paint?"

"I'm not sure what you mean."

"Close your eyes," he said.

Abigail hesitated before complying.

"Now picture this: you walk up to the entrance to Sunset Lodge and are greeted by two large wooden doors. Pulling one open, you enter a small foyer lit by a gorgeous chandelier. The foyer leads you into a spacious living room with a wood burning fire and comfortable seating. Behind a small and very discreet table in the corner, someone checks you in for your stay, handing you an electronic keycard that will open the door to your room."

Abigail opened her eyes. "I quite like this space exactly the way it is."

"The changes I'm suggesting wouldn't cost all that much. We'd add a few walls to make a separate foyer at the entrance and then a few more to make this room smaller and more intimate. Once that was done, you'd have some extra storage space. I'm sure that would be helpful."

"I mean, who doesn't like extra storage space?" Abigail replied.

"I have all sorts of ideas for the kitchen and the dining room, too. I think you should combine them into one huge state-of-the-art kitchen with several small island workspaces. That would allow you to have cooking and baking classes in the kitchen. I'm sure weekend cooking getaways would be very popular."

"That's actually a really good idea," Abigail admitted.

"I can start putting together some rough sketches," Tom offered. "If you'd rather, we could actually start in the kitchen, get those extra workspaces built, and then work on the lobby and foyer later."

Abigail took a deep breath. "I appreciate the ideas, but I'm afraid I simply don't have the budget to make any changes right now. We're painting only because there are already cans of paint in the basement. I'm hoping we'll have enough paint to do every room in the main building. If we can do the annex as well, that will be a bonus."

"The annex? You should really just tear that down," Tom said dismissively. "It's a long rectangular box with no redeeming features."

"I'm not prepared to eliminate six of my guest rooms just yet. I'm really hoping that I'm going to need them at some point."

"How many guest rooms are there in this building?"

"Ten."

"I hate to say it, but I can't see you getting more than ten sets of guests at any one time, not even in the summer. If you do get busy, you would still have the cottages, anyway. I have ideas for those as well."

"I'm sure you do. I really appreciate you taking the time to come and talk to me, but as I said earlier, I can't really afford to do anything right now."

He nodded. "Why don't I take a few measurements while I'm here? I'll just measure the rooms on this floor, and then, when I'm bored at night, I'll play with some ideas."

"I don't want you spending time and effort on planning for things that I may never have done, and I'm not interested in paying you for drawing up those plans."

Tom chuckled. "I wasn't suggesting that you should pay me for my time. I'll be honest with you. I've always wanted to reimagine this space. Jack and Janet weren't interested. They didn't want to change anything about the place where Jack had grown up, and I respected that, but I was hopeful that new owners would be more interested in my ideas."

"It's not that I'm not interested. I simply can't afford to do anything right now."

"Which is why I would love it if you'd let me measure all of the rooms and then start doing some drawings. I asked Jack and Janet to let me measure once, after they'd put the property on the market, but they kept putting me off. I'm asking as a favor, really, because I want to try a dozen or more different ideas. I don't care if you never have me do a single thing."

Abigail frowned. "I can't see the harm in you measuring the rooms, I suppose."

Tom's eyes lit up. "Thank you," he said quickly. He pulled a notebook out of his pocket and then dug in another pocket and removed a small electronic device. "This shouldn't take long," he said as he walked toward the front door.

The phone rang before Abigail could reply. By the time she'd convinced the reporter on the other end of the line that she wasn't going to make any comment, Tom was done with the lobby.

"I hope you don't mind if I do the kitchen and the dining room, too," he said as she put the phone down.

"Of course not," she replied.

As he walked past her, Abigail decided to follow him. He took a few measurements in the hallway before continuing on to the dining room.

"To me, this is mostly wasted space," he said as he worked.

"It's where our guests eat their meals."

"They could do that in a room half this size. That would allow you to substantially increase the size of the kitchen. If you had the guests eat in two sittings, you could make the dining room even smaller."

"Maybe."

Tom looked at her and laughed. "I'm sorry. I'm springing all sorts of ideas on you all at once. I forget that you've only been here a few weeks, whereas I've been thinking about what I'd do if I owned this place for decades."

"You should have bought it."

"I wish," he replied with a sigh. "I thought about it, but a lot of my business is buying properties and then fixing them up and selling them at a profit. At the moment, I'm building a new housing development right outside of town. I had to take out a huge mortgage to buy the land and to start construction, and I won't get any money back until the first houses are built and sold. No bank in the world was going to give me a mortgage to buy this place as well."

"I thought Jack and Janet said the lodge was on the market for over two years."

"It took me three years to buy up enough land for my development," he explained. "The parcel I have now used to be owned by seven different people, and it took ages for me to buy it all."

He took a few more measurements and then shrugged. "Just the kitchen, then."

Abigail followed him.

"Hello?" Marcia said questioningly as they walked into the kitchen.

"Tom is taking a few measurements so that he can draw up some plans for remodeling the lodge," Abigail explained. "I have no intention of doing any such thing, but Tom seems to think it will be fun anyway."

Marcia laughed. "He's been talking about it for long enough. Jack and Janet never wanted to listen to his ideas, though."

"He can hear you," Tom said in an exaggerated whisper.

Both women laughed.

"Right, I think that's all I need," he said a minute later. "Now I can go home and start playing with ideas. I'll do one where we work within the existing walls, one where we take down the wall between the kitchen and the dining room, and a third where we strip the entire ground floor down to the studs and start over."

"We definitely aren't doing that," Abigail said firmly.

"An extension would be useful," he replied thoughtfully. "We could build on to the back of the property, either adding guest rooms or maybe enlarging the kitchen and the dining room. Maybe a sunroom overlooking the lake would be nice."

"The annex is in the way," Marcia pointed out.

"Oh, we're going to tear down the annex," Tom told her. "Maybe we could build a two-story extension. That would give you that sunroom with some guest rooms above it."

"I'll call you when I win the lottery," Abigail replied dryly.

Tom laughed. "Okay, okay, I know. I need to keep my dreams in check. I'll start with a very basic remodel, one that will keep all of the existing walls and simply allow you to use the spaces more efficiently. We won't take down any walls, but we'll add a few..." He trailed off and then grinned at Abigail. "I'm mostly talking to myself. I think I should probably just let myself out now."

Abigail followed him back through the house to the front door. As he reached it, he turned back around.

"I don't suppose – that is, would you like to have dinner with me some time? If I promise not to talk about what I want to do to your building? I'd love a chance to get to know you better."

"Um, okay," Abigail replied, blushing.

"Tomorrow night? I could pick you up around six, and we could drive into Rochester for a meal. I know of a few good places there."

"Sure."

"Italian, Chinese, or Indian?"

"Italian."

"I'll make a reservation, and I'll see you around six tomorrow." Tom gave her a bright smile before turning and letting himself out.

"And now I have a date," Abigail muttered as she walked back to the desk. "With a man who is more interested in the lodge than me," she added with a rueful grin.

She sat down and glared at the answering machine. Its

light was blinking yet again, but she didn't bother to play the messages. Instead, she opened a browser window and started looking for hotels and resorts that offered cooking and baking getaway packages.

"Abigail?"

The word made her jump. She looked around and then smiled at Marcia. "Sorry, I was down a rabbit hole, looking at hotels and inns that offer culinary getaway packages."

"What?"

Abigail laughed. "Tom suggested that we could extend the kitchen and add a few extra workstations and then do cooking and baking classes."

"Who's going to teach those?"

"I thought you could."

"Me? I don't know anything about teaching."

"I won't argue for now," Abigail replied. "I can't afford to extend the kitchen, so there's no point in worrying about it. I will say that such things look very popular, though. It's something to think about for the future."

"Not in my kitchen," Marcia said under her breath. "But that's why I came to talk to you, actually."

"Is there a problem?"

"No, not at all. You asked us to think about ways to help the lodge make some extra money. I think you should call Barry Cuda."

"Barry Cuda?"

Marcia shrugged. "It may not be his real name, but he makes his living on the water, so it suits him."

"And I should call him?"

"He used to run the boat rental place at the Xanzibar. When it closed, he worked for Scott Wright for a few years, running his boat rental business. He and Scott had a falling-out about something, and Barry went back to doing not much of anything besides fishing. I thought maybe you could talk to him about reopening the boathouse here at the lodge."

"I haven't even been inside the boathouse yet."

Marcia nodded. "Jack and Janet stopped doing boat rentals at least ten years ago. Maintaining the boats takes a lot of time and money, and they decided it was more work than it was worth to them."

"I'm surprised the guests didn't complain."

"Some of them probably did, but Scott's place isn't far away, and he used to give us coupons for discount rentals that Jack and Janet could give to the guests."

"I wonder if he'll do that next summer."

"Probably, but you won't want to pass them out if you're going to have your own rentals. I would imagine you'll have to charge more than Scott does in order to make a profit."

Abigail frowned. "I don't even know if I have any boats. Jack and Janet said that there were some in the boathouse, but I have no idea what's there or what condition any of it is in."

"There's only one way to find out."

"Yes, but I don't have a key to the padlock on the door," Abigail told her with a sigh. "Apparently, the key got lost at some point over the past ten years. Jack told me that they hadn't wanted to go into the building, so they didn't pay much attention to the key, not until I asked to take a look around. That's when they realized that they had no idea where the key had been left."

"I'm surprised they didn't find it when they packed their things."

"I was hoping they would, but they didn't." Abigail shrugged. "It's not a problem. I just need bolt cutters or some such thing."

"Barry will have some."

"He will?"

Marcia laughed. "Barry's a character. Give him a call and

ask him to meet you at the boathouse with some bolt cutters. After you see what's in there, you can talk to him about restarting the rentals."

"I'm not sure I can afford to pay him," Abigail said frankly.

"He'd probably be happy to work for a percentage of what the rentals make. He's not all that interested in money. He just loves being on the water. I'll bet, if you call him, he'll be eager to help."

"What happened between him and Scott Wright?"

"I have no idea. You could always ask Scott."

"I might, if I ever meet him."

"He'll be here, sooner or later. I'm surprised he hasn't come and introduced himself already, really."

"Maybe he's really busy at QuackMart," Abigail suggested with a grin.

"Oh, you'll never see him in QuackMart. He has staff that does his grocery shopping for him, and I'm pretty sure they shop in Rochester at one of the big stores there."

"Do you think he'll be upset if we reopen the boathouse?"

"I'm sure he'd rather that we didn't, but he won't do anything to try to stop us."

"Why didn't he buy the lodge?" Abigail asked as the idea occurred to her.

The door suddenly swung open. Abigail smiled at the very handsome dark-haired man who quickly made his way across the lobby. He was casually dressed, but his clothes looked expensive. As he ran a hand through his hair, Abigail noticed a large gold watch on his wrist.

"You could ask him that yourself," Marcia suggested, nodding toward the new arrival.

"Marcia, you look lovely today," the man said smoothly.

"Thanks," she replied. "And now I should go and start working on menus," she told Abigail. "You know where I am if you need me." She nodded at the man and then turned and walked away.

"You must be Abigail Clark," the man said as Marcia disappeared down the corridor.

"I am, yes."

"I'm Scott Wright. It's a pleasure to meet you. Everyone in town was happy to hear that Jack and Janet had found a buyer."

"Why didn't you buy the lodge?" Abigail blurted out.

Scott looked surprised. "That's a tough question to answer," he replied with a small chuckle. He looked around the room and then back at Abigail. "I'm not quite sure how to answer that, actually. I'd be lying if I said that I didn't give the idea some thought, but I suppose it simply came down to me feeling as if it wasn't the right investment for me. Since you asked, I'm going to assume that you know something about me."

Abigail nodded. "I've been told that you own a large percentage of the local businesses."

Scott shrugged. "A few shops and restaurants here and there, a strip plaza or two, a couple of factories on the edge of town, and some other miscellaneous properties. I never intended to own so much, but I love Nightshade, and I do what I can to support the town. Sometimes that means buying businesses that might otherwise go under."

"It's nice to meet you," Abigail replied.

"I assume you have a lot of plans for Sunset Lodge."

"I have some plans, but little money," she replied honestly.

He nodded. "That was another reason why I didn't buy the lodge. It needs a lot of work. The structure is sound, but cosmetically, it needs work – more work than I wanted to put into it."

"But it's beautiful," Abigail replied, waving a hand. "I fell in love with the place when I first walked into the lobby."

"Then I'm sure Sunset Lodge is in good hands, which is great news for everyone in Nightshade."

"We're going to start painting soon."

"Down here or in the guest rooms or both?"

"Both, but down here first. Luckily, Jack and Janet left some cans of paint behind. Hopefully we'll be able to get the entire ground floor painted, at least."

"Are you open to guests now?"

"Yes and no," she replied, smiling as he frowned at her reply. "We are, if someone wanders in off the street, but we aren't advertising that fact. I know we need money coming in because a lot of money is going out every day, but I'd rather not have too many guests before we've gotten at least some of the necessary work done."

Scott nodded. "What about the annex? After what happened out there, what are your plans for that?"

Abigail sighed. "I have no idea. I can't imagine ever putting guests in the room where it happened, but I also hate the idea of losing a room. We don't have all that many as it is."

"Everyone in town is shocked and horrified by Rusty's murder. I can assure you that such things never happen in Nightshade."

"I hope you're right."

"I am," he replied firmly. "Do you know how much longer the police are going to be working in the annex?"

"No. Fred doesn't tell me anything."

Scott laughed. "He may well tell me something if I ask. I'm only curious because I want to help. One of the businesses I own is a cleaning company. One of the things they specialize in is cleaning up biohazard sites, like the room in your annex."

"Biohazard?" she echoed.

He nodded. "Once the police are finished out there, give me a call. I'll send in a team of my best to deep-clean the room for you." He reached into his pocket and pulled out a card case. After extracting a card, he turned it over and jotted something on the back of it with a fancy pen that he'd taken out of another pocket. Then he handed Abigail the card.

"Thanks," she said, glancing at it.

"I put my cell number on the back. I don't give it out very often, but I trust you to use it appropriately. Call me when you're ready to have that annex room cleaned."

"How much will it cost?"

"Consider it a 'Welcome to Nightshade' gift from me," he replied. "I hope to hear from you soon."

Abigail opened her mouth to reply, but the man walked away before she could speak.

Chapter Eleven

The ringing telephone grabbed her attention. "Hello?"

"Ms. Clark? Hello. This is Ross Danielson. I own the *Nightshade News,* our community's local newspaper."

Shoot, can I just hang up on him? Abigail wondered. "Hello," she said as she tried to decide.

"I hope I'm not catching you at a bad time, but I need to speak to you about a number of things."

"No comment," she said flatly.

Ross chuckled. "If you knew how many times each day I hear that – but never mind. If you don't want to talk about how Rusty Morris managed to get himself murdered in your annex, then we can talk about how you can start reversing all of the negative publicity the Sunset Lodge is now receiving."

"Negative publicity? Are we getting negative publicity?"

"I saw a few worrying things on a website in one of the nearby cities."

Abigail quickly turned to her computer and started

searching for the site he'd mentioned. "Where, exactly?" she asked a moment later.

"I'd rather not say. As much as I don't agree with what was said in the article, the site has a right to publish whatever they feel is best."

"Yes, but I have a right to know what's being said about me," Abigail argued.

"And you absolutely ought to be putting out statements of your own," Ross replied.

Abigail closed the window on the computer and sat back in her chair. It seemed obvious that Ross was going to try to persuade her to make a statement. The conversation needed her full attention.

"No comment," she said again.

"Of course," Ross replied. "I often find that suspects in murder investigations are reluctant to make statements to the press."

"I'm not a suspect."

"Of course you are, darling."

"I didn't even know the dead man."

"A little bird told me that your sister knew him very well indeed."

Abigail sighed. "Whether that's true or not, I didn't know him, but that's strictly off the record."

"Why do people always say that?" Ross asked with a sigh. "Regardless, you're still a suspect."

"Why would I kill a random stranger?"

"Maybe you were attracted to him, and he wasn't interested. Maybe he was attracted to you and was too persistent. Maybe he tried to use a stolen credit card. Maybe he stole your credit card. Maybe he liked a football team you hate. The list is literally endless."

"I don't know whether I should laugh or cry at your list."

"Why don't we talk about it over a drink? Charlie's isn't far from the lodge. I'll meet you there in an hour."

"Sorry, I'm not interested."

"You're new in town. I'm sure you could use friends."

"You're a reporter, looking for a story that will sell more papers, not friends."

"I'm always looking for both."

"And the first keeps you from making the second."

"Ouch."

"And now I'm hanging up, but gently, because I don't dislike you. I'm just not going to help you. Please stop calling me."

Abigail put the phone down and then sighed. "I should have stayed in the city," she muttered as she looked at the computer screen. She'd put "Sunset Lodge" into a search engine and found nothing but headlines screaming about murder. Whoever had said that there was no such thing as bad publicity was wrong.

As the phone rang again, Abigail looked at the to-do lists next to the phone. Her personal list was covering up the printed and laminated list that Jack and Janet had left behind. Sighing, she picked up her list and looked at the older one.

"'Clean and prepare empty rooms for incoming guests,'" she read. "That's easy when you don't have any incoming guests. 'Clean occupied guest rooms.' Oh, no, I forgot to clean Amy's room."

She jumped out of her seat and headed for the stairs. After Lisa and Ken left, Amy had gone back upstairs, presumably to her room. Abigail found herself hoping that the woman had gone out again so she could get the room cleaned as quickly as possible. There wasn't any sign on the door, so Abigail quickly grabbed the cleaning cart from the closet and rolled it to Amy's door. She knocked loudly and then counted to a hundred. After knocking again, she pulled out her keys.

As she fitted her key into the lock, she had a sudden flashback to the previous day. *Will I ever be able to open a guest room door and not worry about finding a dead body again?* she wondered as she turned the key.

"Housekeeping," she shouted loudly as she opened the door a crack. "Mrs. Morris? Are you in here? It's Abigail. I've come to clean the room."

After counting to a hundred again, Abigail pushed the door open the rest of the way and switched on the lights. "Hello?" she called loudly, glancing anxiously at the closed door that led to the bathroom. "Is anyone here?"

Before she started cleaning, Abigail opened the door to the bathroom. She felt incredibly relieved to find the small room empty.

Half an hour later, she'd dusted and cleaned and vacuumed everything. She was just checking that she'd put all of the cleaning supplies back on the cart when the room's door swung open.

"What are you doing in here?" Amy demanded angrily.

"Housekeeping," Abigail replied.

"I don't want you in my room."

"Then you should have put the Do Not Disturb sign on the door. I clean every occupied room every day."

"Well, don't clean mine again."

"You're leaving tomorrow, anyway, aren't you?"

Amy frowned. "Probably not, actually. Now that I'm here, I want to stay here until the police have worked out exactly what happened to Russ."

"I'm going to need you to stop at the desk and pay for however many extra nights you plan to stay, then," Abigail told her. She didn't trust the woman to pay when she was leaving.

"I don't know how many nights I'll be staying, do I? It all

depends on how long it takes the police to find out who killed my beloved Russ."

"You can pay for a night at a time, then. Come and see me tomorrow morning to pay for tomorrow night."

"I can't believe you're being so demanding. I'm in mourning."

"And I'm just trying to keep my business afloat."

"You should leave now," Amy snapped back.

Abigail inhaled slowly, counting to ten as she did so. "Dinner is at six," she told the woman as she pushed the cleaning cart to the door. "Spaghetti with salad and garlic bread tonight."

"I may have other plans."

"Suit yourself. Dinner is included in your stay, but we don't offer any discount if you choose to eat elsewhere."

Amy shrugged. "We'll see."

Abigail pushed the cart out of the room. When she turned around to close the door behind herself, Amy shut it in her face.

"Okay, then," Abigail muttered as she returned the cart to the closet. When she got back to the lobby, Carl was sitting behind the desk.

"Sorry, the phone rang," he said as he jumped up.

"I forgot to forward it to my cell," Abigail replied with a sigh. "I'm not used to doing all of the jobs myself."

He nodded. "Jack and Janet always had each other. Jack usually manned the desk while Janet did whatever needed doing in the guest rooms."

"And I was supposed to have Mandy, but she isn't here yet. It will be fine, once I get used to what I need to do and when."

"Good afternoon," a voice said from behind Abigail.

She spun around and smiled at Jessica, who was slowly making her way into the room. "Hello."

"Hi," Carl said. "I better get back to work," he added before he rushed out of the room.

"That was odd," Abigail said as she watched the man leave.

Jessica laughed. "There's something going on between him and one of my third cousins. The whole family is curious, but neither of them is talking. I'm sure he was just afraid I'd start asking difficult questions."

"It's lovely to see you again."

"Thank you, dear. Come, sit and chat with me," Jessica replied. She walked over and settled herself on one of the couches.

Abigail joined her, plopping down on the chair opposite Jessica.

"I've been watching all of the people coming and going from here," Jessica told her. "You've met all of the main suspects in the case now."

"Have I?"

"Of course, I'm simply assuming that you've met everyone who has visited the lodge since Rusty's murder. I suppose it's possible that you were out when some of them were here."

"I don't even know who the main suspects are."

"Everyone I mentioned last time, of course. Oh, they may not be Fred's main suspects, but the more I think about the case, the more convinced I am that one of them is the killer. Of course, you may have your own ideas about who killed Rusty Morris."

"I don't have any idea at all. I didn't know the man or who might have wanted him dead."

"I'm sure you've heard plenty about possible motives now, haven't you?"

Abigail nodded. "Most people seem to think that he was killed because of what happened ten years ago."

"It's the only thing that truly makes sense. He wasn't in town long enough on this visit to lie, cheat, or steal anything."

"Remind me again who you think the main suspects are," Abigail asked.

"Lisa Carter, Ken Carter, Tom Evans, Mark Cooper, or Scott Wright," Jessica rattled off the list. "I'll add Amy Morris to the list, because people are usually killed by the people closest to them, aren't they? I haven't had a chance to meet Mrs. Morris yet, but I'm sure you can tell me all about her."

"I'm not going to gossip about my guests."

"My dear, it isn't gossip. I'm trying to solve a murder. If nothing else, you must consider that you could be in danger if Amy is the killer."

"Me?"

"You're staying in the lodge with her. What if she knocks on your door in the middle of the night and then, when you open the door, she stabs you to death?"

Abigail shut her eyes and took a slow deep breath. "No one is going to stab me to death," she said through gritted teeth.

Jessica leaned forward and patted her arm. "I didn't mean to upset you, my dear. I do want you to think about the possibility, though. I would hate for anything awful to happen to you. I don't know if Amy has an alibi or not."

"She was in New York City the night that Rusty died."

"Are you certain? Maybe she called Rusty and arranged to meet him in his room. Then she killed him and went home again."

"It takes five and a half, maybe six hours to drive from here to New York City."

"You didn't find the body until the afternoon. She could have driven all night."

"She may not have been in New York City," Abigail mused. "I can't remember what time she arrived here yesterday – I can't believe it was only yesterday – but it wasn't six hours after I found the body."

"But she gave you a New York City address when she checked in? Was it the same address that Rusty gave you?"

Abigail frowned. "I think we should leave this to the police."

Jessica hesitated and then shrugged. "There's no harm in talking about the lovely men and women that you've met since you've been here, is there? None of them are guests, anyway."

"I suppose not."

"What did you think of our local family doctor, then?"

"He seemed very nice. He was here when Amy arrived, and he was very helpful when she started crying. She was still in shock, of course."

Jessica nodded. "He's a charming man. I never could understand why he married Sharon Hopkins."

"Oh?"

"They were all wrong for one another. I told my daughter on their wedding day that Sharon would be cheating on him before their first wedding anniversary. She met Rusty about seven months after the wedding."

"And may or may not have had an affair with him."

"And may or may not have crashed her car while on her way to see Rusty."

"You didn't mention that part before."

"Because I didn't know that part before. I made a few phone calls after I spoke to you yesterday. One of the women I talked to was once close to Sharon. When we talked last night, she let it slip that before Sharon left, she'd hinted that she was going to see Rusty on her trip."

"Hinted?"

"My source said that Sharon said something about not coming back to Nightshade. Betty, er, my source, told her that she was crazy to leave Mark, who was making good money and would take good care of her, but Sharon replied that she was going to be meeting up with someone who had a lot more money than Mark, even if some of the gains were somewhat ill-gotten. When Betty asked for more information, Sharon refused to tell her anything."

"And then Sharon died in a car accident," Abigail said thoughtfully.

"If Mark knew that Sharon had been on her way to see Rusty, he'd have even more reason to hate him."

"We don't even know if Sharon actually was on her way to see Rusty. We certainly don't know if Mark knew or suspected anything."

"Which is why he's near the bottom of my list of suspects," Jessica replied. "What did you think of Ken Carter?"

"As a person or as a suspect in a murder investigation?"

"Both."

"He seemed like a nice person, and he was clearly worried about his wife when he came here."

"He adores her and would do anything to protect her."

"Do you think he would have seen Rusty as a danger to her?" Abigail asked.

Jessica thought for a moment. "That's a very interesting question. He may well have considered the man a danger to Lisa. He definitely would have thought of him as a threat to his marriage."

"So he had a strong motive, but he seemed like a very nice man."

"Nice people kill people every day."

"I hope not every day."

"I'm putting Ken near the top of my list," Jessica announced. "But where does Lisa go?"

"I really liked Lisa. She was incredibly polite to Amy, who said terrible things to her."

"Really? Tell me everything."

Abigail shrugged. "Amy seems convinced that Lisa's baby

wasn't Rusty's, but I think she may be more concerned that Lisa might try to sue her for some share of Rusty's estate."

"She ought to be more worried that everyone in Nightshade will sue her."

"Yes, well, Lisa insisted that she didn't want anything from Rusty unless Rusty had left something to Huey. I was surprised that she stayed so nice and polite while Amy kept accusing her of sleeping around, really."

"Lisa is a lovely person who's worked hard to give her son the best possible life. Huey means everything to her. The only way I could see her ever hurting anyone is if she thought Huey was in danger."

"I can't imagine that Rusty was here to try to get custody of his son."

"No, of course not. Lisa is at the bottom of my list. Tom Evans, though, he might be at the top."

"Tom? Why?"

"What did he tell you about his relationship with Rusty?"

Abigail thought for a moment. "Nothing at all. The subject never came up."

"The subject never came up? He was here for a long time."

"He came to talk to me about some ideas he has for remodeling the lodge. Apparently, he tried to talk Jack and Janet into some of them, but they were never interested. He was hoping I'd be more receptive."

"And you never mentioned Rusty? I can't believe he didn't ask you a few questions at least. He and Rusty were very friendly back in the day."

"Neither of us mentioned Rusty while Tom was here."

"I think that's odd," Jessica told her. "Odd and maybe suspicious."

"Or maybe he simply didn't want to talk about it."

"Maybe you need to talk to him again. This time, though, you need to bring up Rusty."

"Maybe. We're having dinner together tomorrow night."

"Oh? Promise me you'll be very careful."

Abigail frowned. "Do you really think he killed Rusty? He seemed awfully nice when he was here."

"He was already near the top of my list, but the fact that he didn't ask any questions or say anything about Rusty when he was here moves him to the very top."

"Maybe he knew that everyone in town would be asking, and he wanted to spare me having to talk about it yet again."

"Maybe," Jessica said skeptically.

"Is that everyone?"

"Everyone except Scott Wright. What did you think of Scott?"

"He offered to have a cleaning crew come and properly clean the room where Rusty died. He said he wouldn't charge me for the service, either."

Jessica nodded. "That's like Scott. He can afford to be generous, but he also truly seems to care about Nightshade. He does a lot of things like that, things that help out other businesses and the people in the town."

"Why would he have killed Rusty, then? Rusty's murder can't be good for Nightshade."

"That rather depends on why Rusty was here, doesn't it? Maybe Rusty was planning to try to scam everyone out of even more money."

"There's no way anyone would have given him money again, is there?"

"I wish I knew. I will say that Rusty could be very persuasive. If he told everyone that their original investments were safe, offered to pay everyone back, even, and then said that he was ready to go ahead with buying the Xanzibar, people might have been willing to back him yet again."

"That's crazy."

"Maybe, but remember that it's been ten years, ten long

years with the Xanzibar sitting empty. It has so much potential. It was such a beautiful hotel. If it reopened, it would be a very good thing for Nightshade."

"Why doesn't Scott Wright buy it, then?"

"As far as I know, he's been unable to find the owners."

"Ah, yes, the mysterious owners. Maybe, if Rusty truly did know who they are, that was why he was killed. Maybe the owners of the Xanzibar want to keep their identities a secret."

Jessica frowned. "That's a very good point, actually. I hadn't thought of that as a motive, but it could be a very strong one, couldn't it?"

"Surely tracking down the owners can't be that difficult, though. I know you said some corporation bought it, but they must have to file reports of some sort, mustn't they?"

Jessica shrugged. "I haven't talked to Scott about the Xanzibar in years, but the last time we talked about it, he said that the company that bought it was just a shell and that he couldn't seem to trace the ownership any further. At that time, he'd just bought one of the strip plazas and wasn't all that interested in buying anything else. He told me he wasn't planning to keep digging."

"Maybe the police ought to do some digging."

"I doubt they've even thought of that as a possible motive."

Chapter Twelve

Marcia stuck her head into the room. "Dinner is ready when you are," she told the pair. "And I made plenty of everything if Ms. Jessica wants to join you."

Jessica grinned. "Jack and Janet used to invite me to join them all the time," she told Abigail. "Marcia always makes too much food."

"I do," Marcia agreed. "But nothing gets wasted, I swear."

"You're more than welcome to join me for dinner," Abigail told Jessica. "Amy might be coming down as well. I'm sure you'd love to meet her."

"Definitely," Jessica replied.

The trio made their way into the dining room. Jessica and Abigail ate large bowls of salad and then steaming plates of spaghetti with meatballs and crusty garlic bread that was dripping with butter and smothered in melted cheese.

"This is my favorite meal of the week," Abigail said as Marcia put a slice of chocolate cream pie in front of her.

"It's one of my favorites," Marcia replied. "I could eat

pasta every day, but I do get tired of having the same sauce every week."

"So start mixing things up," Abigail suggested. "Wednesdays can be Italian night, but you can make whatever you like within that theme."

"Really? I would love that," Marcia said.

"Now is the perfect time for you to experiment," Abigail said. "You need to try different things and see if they take more or less time to prepare and how the cost of the ingredients compares to what you usually make. Do it now, before we start having guests and discover that what you want to make takes twice as long to prepare and doubles our food budget."

Marcia nodded. "It's a lot to think about. I've been making the same things since I started cooking here."

The two women finished their desserts before Abigail walked Jessica to the door.

"I guess Amy wasn't hungry," Jessica said, glancing at the stairs.

"Dinner is available until eight. She still has an hour to come down if she's hungry."

"Thank you for an interesting conversation and for dinner. Now you must try to talk to all of our suspects again, but this time ask some very direct questions."

Abigail raised an eyebrow. "I'm not interested in interfering in a police investigation."

"I'm only trying to help. Fred does his job well, but he's never investigated a murder before. He needs all the help he can get."

Before Abigail could reply, Jessica turned around and headed off down the sidewalk toward the road.

Abigail watched until the older woman disappeared behind the line of trees that ran along the property line between the lodge and Jessica's house. Then she shut the door.

The rest of the evening passed slowly. Amy never came

down for dinner, and Abigail found herself unable to concentrate on anything from her long list of jobs that needed to be done. Eventually, she gave up and played a few rounds of solitaire on the computer before shutting it down.

"Tomorrow is another day," she reminded herself as she climbed the stairs to her room. Arnold was behind the desk. He would let her know if she was needed during the night.

"Good morning," Abigail said tiredly as she walked into the dining room the next morning.

"Good morning," Marcia replied.

"Hi," Carl said.

Abigail walked to the table in the corner and poured herself a cup of coffee. Holding the cup with both hands, she brought it up to her face and inhaled slowly. After a few sips, she began to feel human again.

"I got the waffle maker out this morning," Marcia said as Abigail turned around. "I can make you a plain waffle or an apple cinnamon waffle."

"Apple cinnamon sounds wonderful," Abigail said.

"That's what I had. It was even better than it sounded," Carl told her. "But I'd better get to work. I'm going to finish going through the paint today. So far, I've found six cans that had never been opened. I had some trouble getting the lids off of some of them, but once I did, the paint inside looked fine. Today I'm going to start going through the cans that have clearly been opened, and then I'll start moving everything we can use upstairs."

"Good, great. Once our guest checks out, we can start painting," Abigail replied.

"So you are trying to get rid of me," Amy said from the doorway.

Abigail frowned at her. "That isn't what I said, or what I meant."

"I suppose I'm a terrible inconvenience," Amy replied with a sniff. "I'm sure Russ was, too, arriving without notice and being foolish enough to get himself murdered in one of your guest rooms."

Swallowing a sigh, Abigail gestured toward the table in the corner. "Why don't you get yourself some coffee and have a seat? Marcia has waffles this morning."

"I can't eat. I know I should be hungry, but I simply can't eat. I missed dinner last night. I simply couldn't stop crying. But now, the thought of food makes me feel quite unwell."

Carl got up and walked to the table. He poured a cup of coffee and added some sugar and cream. "Here," he said, holding out the cup to Amy. "This will help. Start with that, and then try to eat something." He turned to Abigail. "See you later, Boss."

Amy took a sip of her drink and then sighed. "I can't possibly eat," she repeated.

"Waffles and turkey bacon," Marcia announced as she returned with a plate full of food. She put it down in front of Abigail and then turned and looked at Amy. "What can I get you? I have plain waffles or apple cinnamon waffles."

"I'm in a bit of a hurry," Amy replied. "I don't really have time to wait for either."

"Take mine," Abigail suggested. "I can wait for Marcia to make more."

She pushed her plate of food across the table and gestured to Amy. "Please," she added.

"I really don't think I can eat," Amy protested as she walked around the table and sat down.

"There's maple syrup, of course, but there's also cinnamon syrup, if you want to try that," Marcia told her. She pushed a small syrup dispenser closer to Amy.

Amy picked it up and poured a small amount on her waffle. She cut a bite and then popped it into her mouth. "It's good," she said, sounding surprised. As Amy poured half of the container onto her waffle, Marcia disappeared back into the kitchen.

"What are your plans for today, then?" Abigail asked after a moment.

"I don't believe they're any of your business," Amy snapped.

"I was just making conversation. We can talk about the weather if you'd rather. It looks like rain."

"But I was going to walk, er, somewhere."

"Take an umbrella."

"I didn't bring an umbrella."

"We have some behind the desk that you can borrow."

"Really? Cool."

As Amy gobbled down her waffles and bacon, Abigail tried to think of another neutral topic to discuss. She was still thinking when Marcia returned with another full plate.

"I must go," Amy said, jumping to her feet. "I'll be back later."

She rushed out of the room before either woman could reply.

"She seemed to enjoy breakfast, at least," Marcia said as she picked up Amy's empty plate.

"It looks and smells delicious," Abigail replied as she poured cinnamon syrup over the waffle.

"I'm going to start looking through recipes after I've cleaned up from breakfast. I don't think we should start changing anything right away, but maybe, once we start having guests, we could start offering more options each evening."

"That sounds as if it could get expensive."

"Maybe, but I was really just thinking of offering different sides, for example. We always have scalloped potatoes with the baked ham, but we could offer guests a choice of those or seasoned rice. That's just an example, but I think a lot of guests would prefer to have some choices for their meals."

Abigail nodded. "Things have changed a lot since Jack and Janet first took over the lodge. People have higher expectations when they travel, and they don't necessarily want to be told what they're going to be having for breakfast and dinner every day. There are a lot more people with food allergies around today as well and people who are vegetarian or vegan. We need to be able to accommodate them."

"I'll start doing some reading and some planning and then we'll talk again. I'm excited about the possibilities, though. Jack and Janet never wanted to change anything."

"I won't be here for dinner tonight." Abigail had almost forgotten about her plans with Tom.

"Oh? Are you doing something special?"

"Tom Evans asked me to have dinner with him."

"Tom's a nice guy and he's really handsome. Have fun."

"I'm sure I will," Abigail said as Marcia turned and left the room.

The waffle was delicious, and after she'd finished it, Abigail briefly considered asking Marcia for a second one. "That would be far too indulgent," she told herself sternly as she got up from the table. "You're eating too much as it is, and not getting any exercise, either, now that you're here. You need to add exercise to your list of things to do every day." *And stop talking to yourself,* she added as she walked into the lobby.

"The gym downtown is nice," Arnold said when she joined him behind the desk.

"You could hear me?" Abigail felt herself blush.

He shrugged. "I didn't mean to eavesdrop."

"It's fine. I shouldn't talk to myself."

He laughed. "I talk to myself all the time. I even ask myself questions and then answer them. But the gym downtown is nice. I work there a few days a week, helping out a few guys who are trying to build muscle. The gym has a lot of great classes for all ages and ability levels as well as all the modern equipment."

"I've never belonged to a gym. Is it very expensive?"

"I can get you a free three-month membership. You can try it out and then see if you want to join."

"That sounds good."

"Another option would be to put a small gym here," Arnold added. "I suggested it to Jack and Janet a few times, but they weren't interested. People expect such things nowadays, though."

Abigail nodded. "Every hotel that I've ever managed had some sort of gym or fitness center. We probably do need to add one here before too long. I don't know where we'd put it, though."

"It doesn't have to be all that large. Maybe we could use one of the rooms in the annex."

Abigail and Arnold exchanged glances. She was pretty sure he was thinking the same thing she was about which room they could use.

"It's something to think about, anyway. You go and get some breakfast. I'm here now."

Arnold nodded and then walked away. She sat down and switched on the computer. It took her only a few minutes to find nearby hotels of the sort that she considered her competition. A quick scan through half a dozen of them revealed that they all had fitness centers, some of them even attached to spas.

"Maybe we should convert the entire annex into a spa," she muttered as she shut the computer down and pulled out her to-do list.

Half an hour later, she was in the office, digging through

another of the boxes of old paperwork. When she heard the front door open, she walked out to the desk.

"Dr. Cooper, good morning," she said brightly, trying not to stare at the handsome man.

"Good morning," he replied. "I was in the neighborhood, so I thought I'd stop and see how you're doing."

"I'm okay. I've discovered that I'm in way over my head, but that hasn't changed my mind about being here – not yet, anyway."

He chuckled. "Is there anything I can do to help?"

"Not unless you can magic up a fitness center for me."

"A fitness center?"

"It's one of the things we're lacking."

"Really? I suppose I never thought about it, but if anyone had asked, I think I would have assumed that you had one. I would also have assumed that it was full of old treadmills that barely worked and maybe a few free-weights, but I would have expected that much."

"Yes, well, we've none of that, and I think we need it. The problem is, treadmills and the like are very expensive."

"I may actually be able to help you there."

"Really?"

He chuckled. "Nightshade Hospital just got a grant to buy a number of new pieces of exercise equipment. The physical therapy department applies for every grant that they can, and they're successful more often than not. I was just talking to the head of the department, and she was telling me that they have a few treadmills and exercise bikes that are only a few years old, and they aren't sure what to do with them. She'd already offered them to the school district, but they got a grant last year that let them replace everything in the middle school and the high school training rooms."

"I would be more than happy with second-hand equipment."

"Do you have a place to put it?"

"I might use one of the rooms in the annex."

"That's a good idea. You could use the room where the body was found, and then you wouldn't have to worry about having guests stay in there again."

Abigail nodded. "We'll have to see what we can do once the police are finished with the space. Assuming I actually have some equipment to put in there."

"I'll see what I can do," he promised. "Anything else?"

Abigail laughed. "That's more than enough for today, unless you want to do some painting."

"Painting? I can help with some painting if you need help. I'm afraid I'm a bit busy during the week, but I can help on weekends."

"I can't ask you to give up your weekends," Abigail replied quickly. "I was just teasing. Carl and Arnold and I are going to tackle the painting, but not until our guest leaves."

Mark frowned. "Is Amy still here? I thought maybe she'd gone by now."

"She's still here. I'm not sure how long she's planning to stay. Obviously, she's more than welcome, but I don't really know why she hasn't gone home yet."

"She doesn't know anyone in Nightshade, does she?"

"I don't think so. She told me she's never been here before, but she did rush off somewhere this morning."

"Interesting," Mark said. He glanced at the clock on the wall and then back at her. "I need to go and visit a little girl with a broken arm. She fell off her trampoline a few weeks back and has been complaining about the cast ever since. If things have continued to improve, I may be able to remove it today."

"How nice for her."

He nodded and then headed for the door. "One of these

nights, we should have dinner together," he said over his shoulder. "I'll call you about the exercise equipment."

He was gone before Abigail had decided how to reply.

She sat down behind the desk and went back to work on the hotel's website. It was coming together, but the pictures that she'd taken weren't great. While a fresh coat of paint wouldn't solve all of the lodge's problems, it was a start, and she was sure it would look better in pictures as well. She walked to the window and stared out at the annex, still surrounded by police tape. It was difficult to get excited about painting and decorating while the police investigation was still ongoing.

"Good morning," a voice said from the doorway.

Abigail spun around and smiled as Lisa and Ken Carter walked into the lobby.

"Hello," she replied.

"I hope we aren't bothering you," Lisa said tentatively.

"Not at all. I was just standing here thinking about all of the work that needs to be done before I can start properly advertising the lodge," Abigail replied.

"Work?" Ken repeated. "I hope you aren't planning on changing too much. Obviously, it's your property. You can do whatever you like, but I think everyone in Nightshade loves the lodge just the way it is."

Abigail nodded. "Unfortunately, the wonderful men and women who live in Nightshade aren't my target demographic. I need to target people who want a weekend or even a week away, right on the lake, not people who already live on the lake."

Lisa chuckled. "We live in Nightshade, and we can't even see the lake from our house. I'd love to come and stay here for a weekend. It's something we've always talked about doing but haven't yet managed."

"I know a few people in town who come out to the lodge

for their wedding anniversaries or birthdays," Ken added. "Jack and Janet sometimes used to give Nightshade residents special deals when the lodge was quiet."

"Did they? That's interesting. I suppose I hadn't really given that idea much thought. But you didn't come here today to talk about how I can best market the lodge, did you?"

The couple exchanged glances and then Lisa slowly shook her head.

"I was wondering if I could maybe see the room where Rusty, um, that is, you know what I mean," she said slowly. "If you don't mind."

"I wouldn't mind, if I could, but the entire annex is still off-limits," Abigail replied. "The police still have police tape around the entire building."

Lisa frowned. "It's silly to even want to see it, really, but I can't help but feel as if it's my last connection to Rusty. I loved him far more than he deserved."

Ken put his arm around her. "He had the entire town fooled. We all thought he was going to reopen the Xanzibar and make us all rich. We didn't realize we were just making him rich."

"I have so many regrets," Lisa said. "I know I broke your heart when I started seeing Rusty."

"I understood, though. He was smart and good-looking, and he seemed so successful. I knew that was what you deserved. I was just a farmer, barely making ends meet on my father's farm."

"You have never been, and will never be, just a farmer," Lisa said with intensity. "You work harder than anyone I know, and you've done amazing things with your father's farm – our farm now. Rusty swept me off my feet with all sorts of fancy promises, but you've proven your love for me every day since the day we met in kindergarten."

Ken flushed. "I fell in love with you when you told me to

get off the swings so you could have a turn," he said with a grin. "And that was it for me."

Lisa looked at Abigail. "I had big dreams," she told her. "I was going to go to college and get a business degree and then work my way up until I was running a Fortune 500 company. I did love Ken, but he didn't fit in with my perfect imaginary future. I wanted to marry a successful businessman and then hire nannies and housekeepers and cooks so that I could sit behind a desk all day making million- or even billion-dollar decisions."

"Things didn't go to plan, then," Abigail suggested.

Lisa laughed. "It turns out I'm nowhere near ruthless enough to run a Fortune 500 company. I'm not even ruthless enough to manage a shop in a shopping mall. That was my first job after college. I was hired as the assistant manager of a clothing store in a mall, and I was terrible at it. Over time, I got a bit better at telling other people what to do, but it never came easily for me. When my mother fell ill, coming back to Nightshade was an easy decision."

"And then she met Rusty," Ken added.

"Oh, yeah, that," Lisa said with a rueful smile. "I came back with no clear idea of what I wanted to do, and then I met Rusty. He offered me a job, managing the Xanzibar, once it reopened, and then he, well, he swept me off my feet, like I said before."

"But he didn't tell you who owned the Xanzibar?" Abigail asked.

"I wish he had," Lisa replied. "Everyone in town still wants to know the answer to that question. But no, he didn't tell me that or much of anything about his plans, really. When I look back now, I realize that we talked about everything and anything, aside from the Xanzibar, but at the time it just felt like we were busy getting to know one another."

"And then he disappeared," Abigail said after a moment.

DIANA XARISSA

"I can't help but wonder if my pregnancy wasn't part of the reason why he ran," Lisa said. "We weren't planning for a baby, and we were taking precautions, but clearly something didn't work properly. Regardless, when I told him, he claimed he was happy, but things were different after that. In retrospect, I should have picked up on the warning signs."

"He should have been excited about the baby," Ken said. "Huey is a terrific kid."

"That's mostly thanks to you, though," Lisa told him. "You've been the best possible father a little boy could ever have."

Ken shrugged. "I'm just doing my best."

"After Rusty left, most of the town was convinced that I was as guilty as he was," Lisa told Abigail. "Ken was one of the few people who stood by me. I pushed him away for months and months until I finally realized that I'd fallen in love with him all over again. We got married two days before Huey arrived."

"And we're working hard every day on living happily ever after," Ken added.

Lisa put her head on his shoulder. "I'm a very lucky woman."

The phone rang, and Abigail sighed as she walked back to the desk. "It's going to be a reporter," she told the couple as she reached for the receiver.

"We'll get out of your way, then," Lisa said.

Abigail nodded. "I'll be happy to let you into the annex once the police are done with it."

"Thank you," Ken replied. "We'll call first next time."

"Sounds good," Abigail told him as she picked up the phone.

Chapter Thirteen

"Thank you for calling Sunset Lodge," she said into the phone.

"Abigail? It's Scott Wright."

"Oh, hi. I was afraid it would be another reporter. I was all ready to say no comment."

Scott chuckled. "I was just calling to see if you knew when you'd have access to the room in the annex that needs cleaning. I'm trying to schedule my cleaning crew for next week, and I'd really like to put you on the schedule. I'm assuming you want the cleaning done as quickly as possible."

Abigail sighed. "I would like to be done quickly, but I have no idea when the police are going to be done out there. Right now, the entire building is wrapped in police tape."

"I can make a phone call and try to get things moving."

"Oh no, don't do that. I can wait. Maybe you could put me on the schedule for the week after next? They'll have to be done with everything by that time, won't they?"

"I would expect so. I don't think they can keep you out of the space once they've finished processing the scene. Do you have a lawyer in town? He or she could probably put some pressure on the police to move faster. They are denying you access to a substantial part of your property and keeping you from renting out those rooms."

"Yes, well, there isn't exactly a line forming for those rooms," Abigail replied. "I can't imagine that we'll suddenly get so busy that I'll need the annex, and I don't really want to rent out those rooms at the moment, anyway. They all need paint and new carpeting at the very least."

"And right now, the police are preventing you from painting and installing that carpeting."

"Technically, yes, but I have a lot of work to do in here before I start working out there."

Scott sighed. "I'm simply trying to help."

"I appreciate that, but I'd rather not do anything to annoy the local police, especially since I've only been here for two weeks, and I've already found a dead body."

"That is rather unusual, but at least you can rest assured that it is hugely unlikely to ever happen again."

"I hope you're right about that."

"So if I can't put you on the cleaning schedule for next week, what can I do to help? What else do you need to get the lodge up and running?"

Abigail thought carefully before she replied. "I really appreciate your willingness to help, but I think I'm okay for now. We're going to start painting next week, and once we get the ground-floor and the second-floor guest rooms done, I'll probably put the website online to see if that will start getting us a few guests. We're heading into winter now, though. I suspect guests may be few and far between until spring."

"You need to find different ways to attract guests. There's a hotel in Corning that does murder mystery weekends, for example."

"I don't want to do murder mystery weekends," Abigail said flatly.

"That was just an example," Scott said after a moment. "Jack and Janet were happy to have the lodge full during the summer months and then mostly empty for the rest of the year. There's so much more you could do with it, though. You're sitting on a gold mine, really."

"Again, I'm surprised you didn't buy it."

He laughed. "Let's talk about why I didn't buy it in more detail over dinner one night," he suggested. "I'm going to be in Texas this weekend, but maybe next weekend?"

"Ask me again when you get back from Texas," Abigail replied. "I hope you have a nice trip."

"Thanks. It's business, but isn't it always?"

He hung up before Abigail could reply.

She put the phone down and then stared at it. *Why is everyone suddenly so interested in getting into the annex?* As far as she was concerned, the police could take their time. She wasn't ready to deal with room 2A yet.

When her stomach started growling, she headed to the kitchen. Marcia was sitting at the small table in the corner with a pile of recipe books.

"I'm making lists," she told Abigail. "Lists of things we could offer as alternatives to our regular menu, lists of things we could try in place of our regular menu, lists of themed meals we could offer if you wanted to do a themed weekend, lists of things I've always wanted to try cooking, but never have, all sorts of lists."

Abigail laughed. "That sounds great," she said as she started to put a sandwich together. "We can sit down and go through them whenever you're ready."

"It may be a while. It might be better if you give me a deadline. Otherwise, I'm probably just going to keep going through cookbooks forever."

"Surely you'll run out of cookbooks eventually."

"I have a library card, and our local library has a huge selection of cookbooks. I could probably do this for months or even years."

"In that case, let's sit down early next month and talk," Abigail suggested. "We aren't going to start changing anything until we've painted, at the very least, but I would like to start offering guests more options once I start doing some advertising."

"Oh, I almost forgot, I've been making lists of vegetarian, vegan, and gluten-free options as well. Those are actually something of a priority, because we want all of our guests to enjoy meals here, even if they have allergies or prefer to not eat meat."

"I'm surprised you didn't already have some of those options."

Marcia shrugged. "Jack felt that we provided a hearty and delicious meal and that anyone who didn't want to eat it didn't have to. He used to say that vegetarians could just eat the vegetables if they didn't want any meat, which worked for some meals, anyway. I don't think it ever occurred to either of them that we might lose business based on the food that was available."

"Or not available," Abigail added.

"Exactly."

The pair chatted about diets and lifestyle choices while Abigail ate her sandwich and a small salad. She washed them down with a glass of lemonade before heading back to the lobby.

"There you are," Amy snapped as Abigail walked into the room. "I've been standing here for ages."

"There is a sign," Abigail replied, gesturing toward the small sign on the desk.

"'I'm temporarily away from the desk. Please call for assistance,'" Amy read. "I saw that, but I know that's the phone number for the phone on the desk here. The last thing I wanted to do was call it and then have to stand here and listen to it ring."

"When I'm away from the desk, I forward that number to my cell phone. If you called it, I would have answered, and then I would have known you were looking for me."

Amy sighed. "How was I supposed to know that?"

Abigail counted to ten before she replied. "What can I do for you?" she asked.

"I'm probably going home tomorrow."

"And you wanted to pay for tonight's stay? Very good. I'll just need your credit card."

"I'll pay you tomorrow when I'm ready to leave. I may change my mind, anyway."

"I did tell you that I wanted to be paid daily to keep things simple."

Amy frowned and then shrugged and dug into her handbag for her wallet. After a minute spent shuffling credit cards, she held one out to Abigail.

The computer took a moment to approve the charge, but once it was confirmed, Abigail handed the card back to Amy. "Is there anything else?" she asked.

"Yes, there is, actually. I'm going home tomorrow, and I don't want to leave without seeing what I came to see."

"What did you come to see?"

"The annex, of course – or rather, the room where my darling husband lost his life. I'm sure that I'll be able to feel his presence in the room. You just have to let me in."

"Unfortunately, the police still have the entire annex blocked off with police tape."

"Bits of plastic tape can't keep me from my quest. If you want to stay outside the police tape, that's fine. Just give me the key to whichever room was Russ's."

"I'm afraid I can't do that. No one is going into any of the rooms in the annex until the police are finished out there."

149

"Yes, yes, whatever. You've proven yourself to be a good little citizen, but now you need to do what's actually right. I need to see that room. I need that closure, if you will. I need to stand where Russ stood, walk where Russ walked, and lie down where Russ laid his head. I know I won't properly be able to recover from my loss until I've done those things."

"Then you're either going to have to wait until the police are finished or go home and come back another time."

"I don't want to wait, and I certainly don't want to come back here, not ever again. I wish you luck with your lodge, but Nightshade is a horrid little town in the middle of nowhere, and once I'm gone, I won't be back."

"Rusty seemed quite fond of it."

Amy laughed. "Russ had big dreams for the Xanzibar, but he very quickly realized that he was never going to be able to accomplish those dreams. Buying it and fixing it up would have cost millions of dollars. I've heard the stories about how Russ got away with half a million dollars. That wouldn't have been enough to even start on the renovations the Xanzibar needs. He was smart to give up on the project before it ever got started."

"If he'd given up on the project, he should have given people their money back."

"I told you, he was cheated somehow, too. He probably would have given the money back if he could have, but someone else took the money – or most of it."

"I hope you've told the police all of this."

"Sure, but I don't think they believe me any more than you do."

"Whatever I do or don't believe, I won't be letting you into the annex until the police give me permission to do so. You may wait here or at home, your choice, but if you wait here, I'm going to ask you to pay on a nightly basis, in advance."

"This hotel is never going to be a success. I just suffered a huge bereavement, and you're treating me like some sort of criminal or something. You should be doing everything in your power to keep me happy. I am your only actual paying guest, after all."

"I'm doing everything in my power to keep you happy. Access to the annex is sadly out of my control. Feel free to call Detective Williams and shout at him about it if you think it might help."

Amy blew out an angry breath. "I am never, ever, ever coming back to Nightshade, and if I do, I won't be staying here," she said before turning and stomping angrily out of the building.

"Thank goodness for that," Abigail muttered as she sat down behind the desk. After a long afternoon spent testing out different fonts for different parts of the website, Abigail found herself rushing up to her room to get ready for her dinner with Tom.

"This isn't a date," she told her reflection. "Okay, maybe it is a date, but it's just a casual date. It isn't anything serious." She touched up her makeup and then combed her hair.

"Thank you for covering the desk for me. Now that I think about it, I should have told Tom that I'd meet him at the restaurant," she said to Arnold when she got back downstairs. "If things aren't going well, it's going to be a long ride back to Nightshade."

"If things aren't going well, call me," he suggested. "I'll have Karen drive up and get you."

"Thank you. I hope it won't come to that."

"Tom is a good guy. You should have fun."

"I hope so."

Abigail took a couple of deep breaths and then slowly paced from one side of the room to the other. The clock on the wall was halfway through the six bongs on the hour when Tom walked in.

"Good evening," he said, giving Abigail a warm smile. "You look lovely. These are for you." He handed her a small bouquet of flowers.

"Thank you," Abigail replied. "I'll just put them in some water. I won't be a minute."

She rushed through the dining room and into the kitchen with the flowers.

Marcia was stirring a large pot. She grinned at Abigail. "How lovely," she said. "Vases are in the cupboard on the left. We used to put fresh flowers in every room when guests arrived, but after more than a dozen vases were broken in a single year, Jack decided that was enough."

Abigail filled a vase with water and dropped the flowers into it. "I'll take it to my room when I get back."

"You look beautiful," Marcia told her. "The green in the skirt matches your eyes almost perfectly."

"Thanks."

"What is Tom wearing?"

"A dark gray suit," Abigail told her. "With a lighter gray shirt and a dark gray tie."

Marcia nodded. "He's a very attractive man."

"He is."

"Have fun."

Abigail felt her heart racing as she walked back to the lobby. *It's just dinner,* she reminded herself as she went.

"I'm afraid I couldn't get a reservation at the restaurant in Rochester, so I got us a table at the Lakeside. I hope that's okay," Tom said as he escorted her out to his car.

"It's fine. I've heard the food there is excellent," she replied.

Tom held her door for her, shutting it carefully when she was safely inside. Then he walked around the car and got behind the wheel. The drive across town took only a few minutes.

They were seated at a table that gave them a view of the lake. Abigail found herself staring at the dark shape that was the Xanzibar Hotel.

"Are you ready to order?" their waiter asked.

"Sure," Abigail said, even though she'd barely glanced at the menu. She quickly ordered something almost at random and then settled back in her seat, her eyes once again drawn to the empty hotel.

"What shall we talk about?" Tom asked as the waiter walked away.

"Everyone in town seems to be talking about Rusty Morris. I hope you didn't lose a lot of money to his schemes," she said, trying not to stare too obviously at him as she spoke.

He flushed. "I think everyone in town was taken in by the man, but that all happened a long time ago. I'd much rather talk about you and why you bought Sunset Lodge."

Swallowing a sigh and feeling as if she'd already told the story too many times, Abigail told him the story of how she came to be the proud owner of her very own hotel. The waiter brought their drinks while she was telling him about her former job and their food while she was explaining why her sister hadn't joined her in Nightshade yet. By the time he brought them dessert menus, Abigail felt as if Tom had barely said two words all evening.

"Your turn," she said after they'd ordered dessert. "Did you grow up in Nightshade?"

He nodded. "It's always been my home, and I can't imagine living anywhere else. Where did you grow up?"

She was still answering questions about her childhood when the waiter delivered her chocolate cake and Tom's apple pie. Tom insisted on paying for dinner, even though Abigail offered to split the bill.

"Well, thank you," she said as they walked back to his car.

"It was my pleasure. I really enjoyed getting to know you better."

"Next time, I want to get to know you better," she countered. "I've told you my entire life story, and I don't know anything about yours."

"Mine is incredibly dull," he laughed. "But I'll give you all the boring details another time."

He pulled into the parking lot for the lodge and then got out of the car and quickly rushed around it to help her from the car. They were halfway to the door when he stopped, his eyes fixed on the annex.

"I almost forgot. I was going to offer to do you a favor that will actually be a favor for me, too."

"Oh? I'm not sure how that works."

He chuckled. "I just bought a property on the edge of town. It's a nice piece of land, but it has a handful of old buildings on the site. None of them are habitable or even usable, so I hired a wrecking crew to come in next week and clear them all away."

"I can't imagine where this is going," Abigail said.

"Sorry. The thing is, I hired them for the entire week, but I won't be ready for them on Monday. I thought, since I'd already paid them for a week's worth of demolition, that I would send them over here on Monday morning. They could tear down the annex for you and it wouldn't cost you a dime."

"Tear down the annex?"

"That is the most sensible thing to do with it. Surely, you weren't planning on using it for guests? The cost of updating and modernizing the rooms probably wouldn't be much less than the cost of building an entirely new building. I'd be willing to bet that I could help you find ways to build a new building for less, actually."

Abigail counted to ten as they crossed the parking lot and

entered the lodge. Then she counted to ten again before she replied. "Thanks for the offer, but I'm not ready to tear down anything yet," she said, her voice calm.

"I'll be wasting a lot of money, having the crew just sit around on Monday until I'm ready," he argued.

"I'm afraid that's not my problem," she said, keeping her tone pleasant.

"I was just trying to help," he replied angrily.

"I appreciate that, but..." She trailed off as the man turned and walked back out the door.

Chapter Fourteen

"Is everything okay?" Arnold asked from behind the desk, getting to his feet as he spoke.

"Everything is fine," Abigail replied. She stood at the door, looking through the window just in time to see Tom driving away. Before she turned back around, she pulled out her keys and locked the door.

"It's a bit early for that, isn't it?"

"Probably, but I thought I may as well, since I'm standing right here." The excuse sounded lame to Abigail's ears, but she didn't want to tell Arnold that something about Tom had made her nervous.

"Sure, okay, if that's what you want to tell yourself. What did Tom do or say to upset you, though?"

"He was trying to be nice," she replied with a sigh. "He offered to lend me a demolition crew to knock down the annex."

"You're getting rid of the annex?"

"No, I'm not getting rid of the annex. He suggested that I should, though, and he got a bit angry with me when I said I wasn't interested."

"Why should he care what you do with the annex?"

"That's a very good question." Abigail shook her head to clear her thoughts. "Do you have any idea where Amy is?" she asked.

"Tucked up in her room. She came down right after you left, and we had dinner together in the dining room. She brought a bottle of wine down with her, and she drank at least half the bottle while she ate. Once we were finished, she went back upstairs to drink the rest and then get some sleep."

Abigail looked at the clock. "Do you want me to take back over until ten?"

He shook his head. "I'm in the middle of a good book, and this chair is quite comfortable. You go and get some sleep. I'll sit here until ten or eleven and then transfer the phones to my cell, then stretch out in the office and get some sleep."

"You know you can go back to your cottage to sleep."

"Yeah, but we have a guest. I'd rather not be that far away while we have a guest."

"Karen must miss you."

Arnold laughed. "Karen is delighted that I'm staying up here at night. Not only do I snore, but I'm also a blanket hog. I always stayed in the office or a room in the annex when Jack and Janet had guests, and that suits my lovely wife just fine."

"Well, you can have a room in the annex again once the police are finished with it."

"Unless you change your mind about tearing it down," he said with a wink.

She laughed. "That isn't going to happen, at least not between now and Monday."

———

"I may be losing my mind," Abigail said to Marcia in the dining room the next morning. She'd already taken several sips of coffee, but the hot liquid hadn't helped with her confusion. "I know I forgot to get my flowers last night, but that bouquet looks much larger than I remember."

Marcia laughed. "Your flowers from last night are still in the kitchen. That bouquet arrived this morning. There's a card in there somewhere."

Abigail found the envelope and carefully removed it. Her name was written neatly across it. *Sorry I got angry last night. The offer is still good. I will call you later. Tom.* Abigail read the message twice and then tucked the card back into the envelope.

"I take it you had a nice time last night, if he sent you flowers this morning," Marcia said.

"It was nice," Abigail replied neutrally.

"Oh, dear. I feel as if there's a story there. You can tell me everything once I've made your omelet."

While she enjoyed her breakfast, Abigail told Marcia about the previous evening.

"It's a very generous offer, even if it is rather odd," Marcia said when she was done.

"It was definitely both of those," Abigail agreed. "I don't really know what to think of it."

"Knowing Tom, he was simply trying to help. And he's already apologized as well." Marcia nodded toward the flowers on the table.

"I still may not go out with him again," she said as she got to her feet.

"Good morning, boss," Arnold said brightly as she joined him at the reception desk. "There's nothing to report from overnight. Even the reporters seem to have stopped calling."

"I suppose that's good news, although I wouldn't mind hearing that we had a guest or two call to make reservations for later in the year."

"Things will pick up once you start advertising."

"I hope so."

As Arnold walked away, the lodge's door opened. Abigail smiled at Jessica as she walked into the lobby.

"How are you today?" she asked.

"Quite frustrated," Jessica replied. "The police should have Rusty's killer behind bars by now. What are they doing all day?"

"I have absolutely no idea."

"Yes, well, they clearly aren't asking the right people the right questions. I've been thinking about everything we've learned so far, and I'm convinced we know enough now to work out who killed Rusty Morris."

"I don't know anything," Abigail protested.

"I'm sure you know more than you think you do. Come and sit with me by the fire and let's talk."

Abigail hesitated for a moment and then shrugged. She didn't really have anything else she needed to do. They weren't going to start painting until Monday, and everything else was contingent on getting the painting done. While she'd been thinking, Jessica had taken a seat on one of the couches. Abigail walked over and joined her.

"If you actually think you know something, you should call Fred," she suggested as she settled back in her seat.

Jessica frowned. "I don't know anything that Fred doesn't also know. But if we put our heads together, I'm pretty sure that we're smarter than Fred."

"He's a trained investigator."

"Who usually investigates joyriding teenagers and a bit of shoplifting. I've been reading murder mysteries for decades. I probably know as much about how such investigations work as Fred does. We just have to look at motive, means, and opportunity."

"We've been through this before. Everyone in town had a motive."

"Yes, or maybe no, but I had a very interesting conversation with Amy Morris yesterday. She told me that Rusty hadn't stolen any money. She said that he'd finally worked out what had happened to the money, and that he'd come back to make things right."

"And you believed her?" Abigail asked.

"No, not at all, but it did make me think. When Rusty left, all of the blame for what happened fell on him. But what if he had a partner here in Nightshade, someone who knew exactly what Rusty was up to and even helped him achieve his aim? That someone might have gotten some money from Rusty before he disappeared. And that someone might have wanted more when Rusty came back."

Abigail thought for a moment. "He could have had a partner here," she conceded. "But if he had, surely Lisa would have known about him. Unless Lisa was his partner."

Jessica shook her head. "Lisa would never have been a party to cheating her friends and neighbors out of so much money. She's still at the bottom of my list of possible killers, but she's not on the possible partner list at all."

"You think she might murder someone, but wouldn't steal? That doesn't make sense."

Jessica shrugged. "I can make my list of suspects my own way. I'm trying to focus on who might have been working with Rusty. Lisa isn't on that list for me, but you may put her on your list, if you truly think she might have helped Rusty defraud everyone in the town of Nightshade, the town where she grew up and where she continues to live to this day."

Abigail frowned. "When you put it that way, it seems unlikely that Lisa was involved, but the same is probably true for everyone who still lives in town, isn't it? If Rusty did have a partner here, surely he or she left some time after Rusty did."

"Maybe, but what if Rusty's partner stayed right here, waiting for Rusty to return? Maybe the partner knew that

Rusty would be back. Maybe the partner has control of the money and knew that Rusty would be back because he was going to want his share?"

Abigail shook her head slowly. "This is all getting far too complicated."

"Never mind all of the finer details, let's focus on the suspects. We've already talked about Lisa and discounted her. What about Ken?"

"Rusty stole Lisa away from Ken. I can't see him working with Rusty on anything."

Jessica nodded. "You're probably right about that, but I'm still keeping him on the list. He's at the very bottom, though. If he had worked with Rusty on the scheme, I don't think he'd have managed to keep his mouth shut about it for the past ten years."

"That's a good point. If Rusty did have a local partner, he or she has kept quiet about it for a long time. Is there anyone in town who lives far above his or her means?"

"That's an interesting question. Lisa and Ken certainly don't. They both work hard on the farm, and I can't remember them ever taking a vacation or buying anything extravagant."

"Scott takes plenty of vacations," Abigail said slowly.

Jessica laughed. "Scott makes more than enough of his own money. He doesn't have to steal from anyone."

"So you don't think he was Rusty's partner?"

"I can't see Scott actually working with Rusty on anything. I don't know that I've ever heard of him having a partner on any project. He did do a lot to support Rusty's plans, especially in the early days, though. Still, I find it hard to believe that he knew what Rusty was really doing. Half a million dollars is pocket change to Scott Wright."

"Really?"

Jessica laughed. "I'm exaggerating, but the man does very

well with his businesses. He doesn't need to cheat people out of their money, even if he does overcharge for everything in QuackMart."

"So he isn't on your list of possible partners for Rusty?"

"He can go under Ken on the list. We should talk about Mark Cooper, though."

"Dr. Cooper?"

"He bought a nice big house and a brand-new car not long after Rusty left," Jessica said. "That was right after his wife died. He told me that he'd received a large insurance payout after her death."

"But you didn't believe him?"

"I believed him at the time, but now I'm wondering. Is it possible that he was working with Rusty?"

"I thought you said he didn't like Rusty. Didn't you say that Mark's wife had an affair with the man?"

"There was talk, but no one had any proof. What if Mark and Rusty started the talk so that no one in town would realize that they were actually close friends who were working together?"

"I suppose that's possible, but I can't see why Mark would partner in a scheme to steal money from people. He's a doctor. He's supposed to be one of the good guys."

"I like him a lot," Jessica told her. "I don't want to believe that he was working with Rusty, but I have to admit that it's possible."

"I think Tom is more likely," Abigail said thoughtfully. "He's a contractor, so it would make sense for Rusty to reach out to him to talk about the work that needed to be done at the Xanzibar."

"And Tom would have been thrilled. He loves restoring old buildings."

"He wants to completely change this one."

"Does he? I'm sure he thinks he'll be improving things."

"He does, but I'm not ready to start tearing out walls or adding new ones, either."

"Can we think of anyone else who might have worked with Rusty?"

"I can't, but then I don't know very many people in Nightshade."

Jessica nodded and then sat back in her seat. She shut her eyes and began to breathe in and out slowly. Abigail watched her for a minute and then frowned. She had things to do.

"I need a moment or two," Jessica said. "You go and get some work done or something."

Frowning, Abigail got up and walked back to the desk. She worked her way through a day's worth of emails, deleting nearly every one of them.

"The annex is the key," Jessica said suddenly, making Abigail jump.

"What do you mean?" Abigail asked as she walked closer to the woman, who was sitting up and looking around the room.

"I mean, why did Rusty want a room in the annex?"

"Because he wanted to be able to come and go as he pleased? Or maybe he wanted to be able to park his rental car right outside of his room."

"Or maybe he wanted to be able to meet with someone without anyone noticing," Jessica said. "Sadly, that's exactly what happened, which is what brought us to this point."

"Everyone is obsessed with that stupid annex at the moment."

"What do you mean?"

"Everyone involved with the case has asked me about the annex in the past twenty-four hours or so. Lisa and Amy both want to see the room where Rusty died. Ken came with Lisa to ask, actually. Mark wants to help me turn that room into a fitness center. Scott wants to help me get it properly cleaned, and Tom wants to demolish the entire building."

Jessica frowned. "Interesting." She sat back and shut her eyes again.

Is it, though? Really? Abigail wondered as she walked back to the desk. She watched Jessica for a short while. The woman was breathing slowly and deeply, and Abigail began to suspect that she'd fallen asleep. Deciding it didn't really matter, Abigail answered the two emails that hadn't been junk and then started going back through the budget spreadsheets that Jack and Janet had left her. She and Mandy had glanced through them before they'd bought the property, but this was the first time that Abigail went through them line by line. After a few minutes, she dug out a notebook and started taking notes.

"We're going to have to call them both," Jessica's voice cut through the quiet. "One of them will confess, once we've pushed him."

"What?"

Jessica opened her eyes and looked at Abigail. "I've thought it all through and I know who killed Rusty."

"Excellent, call Fred and tell him all about it."

"I could, but that would take far too long. He has all sorts of rules and regulations to follow. The killer was quite careful, or else Fred would have arrested him already. That means we have to outsmart him."

"So who do you think killed Rusty?" Abigail asked.

Jessica frowned. "I've narrowed it down to two people. It was either Scott or Tom, but I'm not sure which one is guilty."

"What makes you think it was one of them?"

"The biggest red flag is that they both want to do things in the annex."

"They aren't the only ones."

"No, but they are the only ones who want to do something that will destroy all evidence of the murder," Jessica pointed out.

"Scott is simply trying to help, and Tom just wants to remodel everything."

"Maybe, or maybe one of them wants to destroy something that he's worried the police might find."

"The police have been through Rusty's room many times over."

Jessica waved a hand. "It isn't just that. Tom came to see you right after the murder and didn't ask you about it. What did he say about Rusty when you had dinner last night?"

"Nothing much. I asked him if he'd lost a lot of money to the man, and he said he thought everyone in town had, and then he changed the subject."

"So he doesn't want to talk about Rusty, and he wants to demolish the annex."

"Neither of which proves anything."

"They were friends when Rusty was here, or at least friendly. He's at the top of my list."

"I'm sure Fred would love to hear your thoughts."

"But Scott is on the list, too. You said he wants to help you clean the room where the body was found?"

"He's offered to send in his specialist cleaning crew to get the room properly cleaned."

"If I were the suspicious type, I'd wonder why he even has a specialist cleaning crew."

Abigail made a face. "I'd hate to think."

"Scott is a very busy man. He works hard and he travels a great deal. I don't know that he visited Jack and Janet more than once or twice a year, and yet he's been here how many times since you bought the property?"

"A few."

"Which means either he's interested in you, or he killed Rusty and he's trying to keep an eye on the investigation."

Abigail laughed. "There are dozens of other things that might explain his behavior."

"Maybe, but those two are the most likely. He wasn't friendly with Rusty when Rusty was here, but he did invest in Rusty's business. Scott prides himself on being a smart businessman. I'm sure he was more than a little angry when he found out that he'd been conned."

"It's a big leap from angry to murder."

"It's always possible that Scott lied about losing money to Rusty," Jessica said thoughtfully. "Maybe the whole con was his idea and he simply hired Rusty to come into town and run the scheme. After Rusty left, Scott was quick to tell people that there wasn't any point in going after the man. According to Scott, the contracts that we all signed were unbreakable. Maybe that was because he had a hand in their design."

Abigail sighed. "All of this speculation is interesting, but pointless. I'm sure Fred is pursuing all avenues."

"And if we sit around and wait for Fred to finish, we'll both go to our graves wondering who killed Rusty Morris. I don't have time to wait for Fred to ask a few questions and then contemplate the answers. We're going to solve the case for him this afternoon."

"We're going to what?"

Jessica chuckled. "My dear girl, I have a plan."

Chapter Fifteen

"**A**bsolutely not," Abigail said firmly after Jessica told her what she was planning. "If you're right, we'd be confronting a killer. If you're wrong, we'd be upsetting two men, both of whom have been nothing but helpful and friendly since I got here."

"One of them killed Rusty," Jessica insisted. "And he may kill again if he isn't stopped soon."

"Even if you're right, and I'm not agreeing that you're right, but even if you're right and one of them killed Rusty, he doesn't have any reason to kill anyone else."

"You say that as if you know exactly what his motive was for Rusty's murder. If it was about money, then Amy might be his next target, assuming she is Rusty's heir, of course."

"She seems to think she is."

"Of course she does. I am rather hoping that he left something to his son, not because Ken and Lisa need the money, but because it would make Lisa and Huey feel as if the man actually did care, at least a little bit."

Abigail nodded. "It was lovely seeing you again. Please drop by any time."

Jessica stared at her for a moment and then sighed. She slowly got to her feet. "I shall have to do it on my own, then," she said as she began to shuffle toward the door. "I hope you won't mind if I call you before each man arrives to speak to me. That should help the police work out which one of them killed me, I hope."

"Don't be silly. You shouldn't be getting involved in a police investigation. Neither of us should be getting involved in a police investigation. Let Fred do his job."

"I can tell each of them that I saw his car drive past my house on the night of the murder," Jessica said, seemingly ignoring Abigail. "It's not as good as you telling them that Rusty mentioned their name, but it may be good enough to worry one of them. Of course, I'll want to tell them in person. I do hope it won't be too much bother, tracking down Scott."

"I'm very easy to find," Scott said from the doorway.

Abigail jumped and then frowned at Jessica. The older woman had walked no more than a few feet away from the fireplace before stopping, and they'd both had their backs to the door while they'd been talking. *How much did he hear?* Abigail wondered as Jessica spoke.

"Scott, my dear, we were just talking about you. How are you today?"

Scott smiled and then walked over and gave Jessica a quick hug. "I'm very well, thank you. I was driving past, and I thought I'd stop and see how Nightshade's newest resident was doing." He looked at Abigail and smiled.

"I'm fine," she replied.

"She's incredibly eager for the police to finish in the annex," Jessica told him.

I have a crew ready to thoroughly clean the room where the body was found," he replied.

"That's very kind of you," Jessica said. "Do you often need the services of a crew like that?"

Scott stared at her for a moment and then laughed. "In a town as old as Nightshade, they spend a lot of time cleaning up sewage," he told her. "Our sewer system is getting older, and there are a number of older houses in one neighborhood in particular that has a lot of problems with sewage backing up into their basements," he said to Abigail. "My crew is the only one in the area that specializes in that sort of cleaning."

"That and dead bodies," Jessica suggested.

"People die in their homes every day. Most families don't have the first clue how to clean up properly after that sort of tragedy," Scott explained.

"Abigail was just telling me that Rusty mentioned wanting to see you while he was here," Jessica said.

Abigail opened her mouth to reply but found herself speechless. Before her brain could work out what to say, Scott shrugged.

"He may well have wanted to see me. I spoke to his widow the other day and she told me that he was hoping to resurrect the Xanzibar project. She seemed to think that he could get everyone's money back and then get more people to invest in the project. I think that would have been a tough sell for the good people of Nightshade, but I can see Rusty giving it a try," he said.

"But then someone murdered him before he had a chance," Jessica said sadly.

"There were still a lot of people in Nightshade who were angry with him," Scott replied. "I suspect Fred is going to need weeks to interview everyone who hated the man."

"Including you," Jessica suggested.

"I didn't hate him," Scott said with a small chuckle. "I did lose some money to his con, but no more than I could afford to lose. I invested to help support the community, but I fully expected to lose the money. I couldn't see Rusty remodeling and running the hotel successfully. As it was, he never bothered to try, and I got to watch my investment disappear in one huge burst rather than watch the money dwindle away as Rusty ran the company out of business."

"Would you have given him even more money?" Jessica asked.

"That depends on the circumstances. If he'd done as Amy suggested he was planning to do, then I might have been tempted. I guess now we'll never know," he replied.

"I don't know when the police are going to be done with the annex," Abigail said as the conversation stopped. "I'll call you."

Scott grinned at her. "I'll look forward to it," he said. "Nice to see you again," he said to Jessica before he turned and walked out of the room.

"How could you do that?" Abigail demanded as the door swung shut. "If he is the killer, you've made me his next target."

"He isn't the killer," Jessica replied.

"Just because you don't think he's the killer, doesn't mean he isn't the killer."

"He would have reacted differently to my questions if he'd done it," Jessica said confidently.

"Abigail? I found this in the basement. I'm not sure what it was doing there," Carl said as he walked into the room. He was carrying a can of paint.

"I thought there was a lot of paint in the basement," she replied.

He nodded. "But it's all beige. This is hot pink."

Abigail looked at the can that was clearly marked "Flamboyant Flamingo" across the top. "Maybe Jack and Janet bought it by mistake."

"Or maybe they used it in one of the hidden rooms," Jessica suggested.

"There are hidden rooms?" Abigail demanded.

Jessica and Carl exchanged glances.

"No," Carl replied after a moment.

"I've heard all sorts of rumors over the years..." Jessica began.

"Ah, hi," Tom said from the doorway. "I hope this isn't a bad time."

"Not at all," Jessica replied. "We were just talking about you."

"Be quiet," Abigail hissed as she took a step closer to the man. "I was just telling Jessica about the lovely flowers you sent. Thank you."

Tom flushed. "You're very welcome. I felt bad about last night. I felt like I messed everything up at the end."

"Not at all. You were simply trying to help," Abigail replied.

"But the last thing Abigail wants to do is tear down the annex," Jessica interjected. "She needs those rooms if she's going to make a profit here."

Tom sighed. "She could charge a lot more for nice rooms in a brand-new building."

"But she can't afford that," Jessica replied.

"I could help, though. I'd be happy to help with the design and find good people who wouldn't charge too much to do the work. That annex really needs to go," Tom said, his voice getting louder as he spoke.

Carl frowned. "Are you okay?" he asked Tom.

"I'm fine. I'm sorry. You all know that remodeling this building has always been my dream. In those dreams, though, the first thing that happens is the annex gets demolished. It's a horrible, unsightly box that takes away from the beauty of this old house," Tom replied.

"Maybe we could do something to it to make it more attractive," Abigail suggested.

Tom shook his head. "It wouldn't be worth what it cost."

He took a deep breath. "I'm sorry," he said again. "I really am just trying to help."

"I saw Rusty the night he arrived," Jessica blurted out. "He told me that he was going to see you later that evening."

Abigail frowned as all of the color seemed to drain from Tom's face. She'd hated when Jessica had lied about what Rusty had told her, but this was just as bad. If Tom was the killer, Jessica was making herself a target.

"Did he?" Tom said after a moment. "I didn't know you saw him that night."

"I saw his car drive past. I wasn't sure that I'd recognized him, but as soon as I realized who I'd seen, I walked over to talk to him," Jessica replied. "I told him that I was going to be calling the police as soon as I got home."

"You should have," Tom told her.

Jessica nodded. "I was foolish enough to let that man convince me to give him twenty-four hours to make everything right. He told me that he was going to talk to you and that together you were going to fix everything."

There was another awkward pause. Abigail could see the effort it was taking for Tom trying to work out how to reply.

"I should go," was what Tom finally said.

"What did Rusty have planned?" Jessica asked. "I assume you knew he was coming."

"I didn't know anything," Tom said, sounding a bit desperate as he turned away.

"But you were Rusty's closest friend when he was here," Jessica replied. "Surely you knew he was coming back to town. He told me that you'd arranged to meet. Did you have a chance to talk to him before someone killed him?"

Tom hesitated and then slowly shook his head. "No, I, we, that is, I never saw him."

"But you did have plans to meet," Jessica said. "I hope you

told the police about those plans. That might help them pin down the time that Rusty died."

"I told the police everything," Tom told her. "But now I have to go."

"Would it be terribly expensive to replace my front porch?" Jessica asked.

Abigail stared at her. *That came out of left field,* she thought.

"What?" Tom asked, clearly feeling much the same way.

"My front porch, on my house. It's getting older, and I was thinking about replacing it. You must do little jobs like that all the time. I was hoping you could give me a ballpark estimate on what it would cost," Jessica explained.

"I'd have to measure the existing porch and then we'd need to talk about some of the different options before I could give you a price," Tom said.

Jessica nodded. "If you aren't busy right now, maybe you could take a quick look, then."

Tom frowned. "I'm afraid I have to be, um, somewhere else."

"Let me give you my number," Jessica said. "Call me when you have a few spare minutes so we can talk. I'll make a cake. Do you prefer tea or coffee?"

"Um, coffee," Tom told her. "But I really have to go now."

"Just let me write down my number," Jessica said, opening her purse. She dug through it for a moment while everyone watched before Abigail snapped out of her daze.

"I have paper and a pen," she said, crossing to the reception desk. She grabbed a pile of sticky notes and a pen and then walked over to Jessica.

"Thank you, my dear," Jessica said. She took them and then very slowly began to write.

"I really need..." Tom began.

"I'm hurrying," Jessica insisted. She looked up and then

shrugged. "I haven't given anyone my number in a long time. I'm afraid I've forgotten it. Let me think."

"Give it to Abigail," Tom told her. "I'll stop back another time and she can pass it along to me. I really have to go."

He crossed to the door and pulled it open. Fred smiled from the doorway.

"Going somewhere?" he asked.

"I have an appointment," Tom told her.

"Do you now? Where and when?" Fred asked.

"In my office in about twenty minutes."

"And who are you meeting?"

Tom frowned. "I don't think that's any of your business."

"It might be my business, if you were meeting with, oh, let's say Rusty Morris's widow," Fred replied.

"It's only natural that I would want to offer her my condolences," Tom argued.

Fred raised an eyebrow. "I think we should talk in my office."

"Why? I haven't done anything wrong," Tom insisted.

"Ask him where he was the night of the murder," Jessica said, taking a few steps closer to the two men. "He knew Rusty was coming back to Nightshade. The two were planning to meet that evening. He and Rusty were partners. He helped Rusty steal from everyone in town."

"Those are some pretty serious allegations," Fred said.

"She's crazy," Tom shouted. "I wasn't Rusty's partner. He stole from me, the same as he stole from everyone else."

"Rusty came back to make things right," Jessica said. "He was going to give back the money he took, and he was going to buy the Xanzibar. But he needed you to agree, because you took half of the money."

Tom stared at her for a moment and then started to laugh. "You actually believed that story? I told Rusty no one was going to believe anything that he said, not after what happened ten years ago, but you actually believed his lies, yet again. He insisted that people are stupid. I guess he was right."

"When did you talk to Rusty?" Fred asked.

Tom frowned. "He called me a few weeks ago. He said he was thinking of coming back to Nightshade for a second go. He was sure that he'd be able to convince everyone that what had happened ten years ago had been nothing but a big misunderstanding and that he was now ready to buy the Xanzibar and make it a success."

"At which point you should have called me," Fred said sternly.

"As far as I knew, Rusty hadn't broken any laws," Tom countered. "I thought Scott Wright had Quail investigate, and I thought Quail said that everything that Rusty had done was legal."

"Legal, maybe, but not nice," Jessica muttered.

Tom shrugged. "I did my best to persuade Rusty to stay away. I can't help it if he ignored my advice."

"Why did you want him to stay away?" Abigail asked. "Surely, if he was interested in coming back to Nightshade and buying the Xanzibar, you should have been happy."

"I would have been, if I'd thought he could be trusted," Tom explained. "But I knew better. He was coming to con people a second time. I told him not to do it."

"It sounds as if you knew a lot about Rusty's plans," Fred said. "Let's talk about that in my office."

Tom shook his head. "I've already told you everything I know. Rusty called me out of the blue and said he was thinking of coming back to town. I told him that he'd be wasting his time. I thought that he took my advice and gave up on the idea until, well, until after."

"After what?" Fred demanded.

"When I heard that the body had been found, then I knew that he'd come in spite of my advice," Tom told him.

"Rusty said he was here to meet someone," Abigail interjected. "Who might he have been meeting?"

"I've no idea. I didn't know he was coming. I don't know anything," Tom said. He looked around the room and then at Fred. "I need to go."

"Where were you the night Rusty was murdered?" Jessica demanded.

Tom stared at her for a moment. "Home, alone," he said eventually. "I finished work around six or seven and then I went home, and I didn't go back out until morning."

Jessica nodded. "I'm sure you know Mrs. Stokesbury. She lives across the street from you. You won't mind if I ask her if she noticed you going in and out that night."

"I had to get groceries," Tom said quickly. "After I got home from work, I realized that I didn't have anything to eat, so I went back out and got some groceries."

"Tom, we all know that you saw Rusty that night," Jessica replied. "You may as well admit to it. Maybe you saw or heard something that will help the police work out who killed Rusty. You do want to help your friend, don't you?"

"He wasn't my friend," Tom said flatly.

"Did you bump into him at the grocery store?" Jessica asked.

Tom hesitated and then nodded slowly. "He was at the store, buying some beer to take back to his room."

"Did you give him a ride back here?" Jessica asked. "That would have been the nice thing to do."

"I did, yes," Tom said.

Abigail knew the man hadn't thought through what he was saying. At any moment, he was going to realize that he'd walked into a trap.

"And then you had a lovely chat, didn't you?" Jessica asked in a friendly tone.

"We talked," Tom replied flatly. "And then I left."

"Because it was far too early," Jessica said thoughtfully. "Did you arrange to go back later, or did you decide to surprise him?"

Tom shook his head. "I didn't go back later. I never saw Rusty again after that."

"Of course you went back later," Jessica said with a wave of her hand. "You were angry and upset and sitting at home only made it worse. You went back to confront the man who'd stolen so much from you. The big question is, did you accidentally witness the murder?"

"I didn't go back, and I didn't see anything," Tom insisted. "I was angry, but I stayed home and drank some beer and watched an old movie. I never saw Rusty again."

"What old movie?" Fred asked.

Tom looked at him and then shrugged. "I forget."

Jessica sighed. "You know Mrs. Stokesbury saw you going out again."

"She didn't," Tom insisted. "I went out the back door."

As soon as the words left his lips, his face drained of color. Before he could speak, Fred held up a hand.

"We need to have this conversation in my office after I've read you your rights," he said. "Don't say another word."

"I'm disappointed in you, Fred," Jessica said. "You could have let me get the entire confession. We all know that Tom killed Rusty."

"He knew I was doing well," Tom said, his voice flat. "I'd invested my share of the money and used some of it to build my business. Rusty had simply squandered his share on traveling and women. He started blackmailing me about a year ago. At first the demands were almost reasonable, but they kept getting bigger every month. And then he decided to come back to Nightshade to try to scam everyone a second time. I needed to protect myself and everyone in Nightshade."

"You should have come to me," Fred suggested.

"He had evidence that I'd profited from the original con," Tom told him. "He told me that all of the evidence is in a safe in New York City and that his wife would know what to do with it if anything happened to him."

"But you didn't believe him?" Jessica asked.

"I decided that I didn't care anymore," he told her. "The blackmail was bad enough. That night he told me that he expected me to help him steal from everyone a second time. Ten years ago, I was young and stupid. Making money mattered more than anything. Now, though, Nightshade matters to me. The people here matter to me. I would have kept paying him forever if he'd stayed away. Once he came back, though, he was a threat not just to me but to everyone and everything that matters to me."

"Let's go down to the station and get all of this in writing," Fred said. "You can call Quail or someone else when we get there."

"Dove is best for criminal cases," Jessica told Tom. "I'll call her and have her meet you at the station."

"Whatever," Tom said with a shrug.

Fred put a hand on his arm and led him out of the room. As the door shut behind the two men, Abigail turned and looked at Jessica.

"That was a very dangerous thing to do," she said.

Jessica looked up from her cell phone and smiled at her. "Yes, dear, of course, but once we'd eliminated Scott from consideration, I knew that Tom had done it. I simply had to get him to admit to it."

"He might have killed you, too," Abigail replied.

"He isn't a killer, though, not really," Jessica replied. "Rusty was blackmailing him and planning to cheat everyone in town a second time. I can understand why Tom killed him."

"He should have gone to the police," Carl said.

Jessica nodded. "Well, yes, of course, but if he had, he

would have had to admit what he'd done ten years ago. Obviously, he didn't want to do that."

"I can't believe he killed Rusty," Abigail said, shuddering. "I had dinner with him last night."

"He's a lovely man," Jessica told her. "He made a small mistake ten years ago, and then he made a much larger one a few days ago. I suspect he'll spend the rest of his life in prison, wishing he could go back in time and not make that first mistake."

Before Abigail could reply, Jessica began to speak into her cell.

"Ah, yes, Dove, it's Jessica Fleming. Fred has just taken Tom down to the station. He's more or less confessed to killing Rusty Morris…"

Carl opened the door for Jessica as she wandered out, still talking to the lawyer.

"I texted Fred as soon as Tom arrived," he told Abigail as he shut the door. "Jessica saw what I'd done and did her best to keep Tom here until Fred could arrive."

"Thanks?" Abigail replied, unable to stop herself from making the word a question.

"You still haven't told me what you want me to do with the pink paint," he said.

———

Two weeks later, Jessica paid Abigail another visit.

"I just wanted to make sure you'd heard all of the latest news," she said as she settled herself on one of the couches.

"I haven't heard anything," Abigail replied. "I've been checking the local newspaper's website every day, but they haven't posted anything since the article about Tom's arrest and the note that Amy had left town."

Jessica nodded. "The police will be having a press conference later to announce that Tom has confessed to Rusty's murder."

"I feel kind of bad that he killed Rusty because he wanted to stop him from conning everyone in town again."

"Don't feel too bad," Jessica told her. "Tom wasn't being altruistic, not entirely at least. Rusty's murder was all about money."

"Oh?"

"It turns out that Rusty and Tom were partners in the company that Rusty created. When he left town, he left all of the money in an account to which both he and Tom had access. Over the past ten years, Tom has slowly emptied that account, presumably hoping that Rusty would never come back."

"That wasn't very smart."

"No, not at all. I gather Tom is now claiming that he killed Rusty in self-defense."

"I'm not sure he'll persuade a jury to believe that."

"That wasn't the surprising news."

"Is there some surprising news, then?"

"Just a bit," Jessica said, teasingly.

"Go on then," Abigail said after a long pause.

"Rusty's will has been released. He left half his money to Amy and the other half to Huey. There are a lot of people all over the US who were conned out of money by the man, so Huey may not end up with much of anything, but Lisa is happy that he finally acknowledged his son."

"I wouldn't call that a happy ending, exactly, but it's better than nothing," Abigail said.

Jessica laughed. "Happy endings are for fairy tales, not real-life murder investigations."

The Body in the Boathouse

A SUNSET LODGE MYSTERY

Release date: January 19, 2023

When Barry Cuda arrives at Sunset Lodge to talk to Abigail about running a boat rental business for her, she's eager to take a look at exactly what watercraft is left in the boathouse that's been locked up for over ten years.

Neither she nor Barry is expecting to find a skeleton inside one of the boats. When Barry thinks he recognizes something that's been left with the body, things don't seem to add up.

It doesn't take the police long to identify the remains and they're fairly certain the dead woman was murdered. Abigail can only hope that another murder investigation won't interfere with the special Halloween weekend she has planned for her first group of guests. When Barry offers to supply a group of actors to tell ghost stories on Halloween, Abigail is quick to agree.

But the Nightshade Players all knew the woman who was murdered and Abigail's neighbor, Jessica, is convinced that one of them killed her. Can Abigail get through Halloween night without Jessica sticking her nose right into the middle of another murder investigation?

A sneak peek at The Body in the Boathouse

A Sunset Lodge Mystery
Release date: January 19, 2023

Please excuse any typos or minor errors. I have not yet
completed final edits on this title.

Chapter One

"Maybe this isn't a good time," the man in the doorway said
hesitantly.

Abigail Clark put her hand on the top of the ladder and
then slowly turned to face him. "Hi," she replied. The new
arrival was an older man, at least sixty in Abigail's estimation.
He was wearing jeans and a sweatshirt stretched over a
rounded tummy. Both items looked as if they hadn't seen the
inside of a washing machine in some time. Thick gray hair
matched the long beard that gave him the appearance of a
disreputable Santa.

He looked around the room and then back at her.
"Someone told me you were looking for me."

Abigail frowned and then put her paintbrush in the can of paint that was precariously balanced on the rung above her. She picked up the can and then slowly climbed down the ladder. "Sorry, I can't talk from up there. Someone told you that I was looking for you?"

The man shrugged. "If you're the new owner of Sunset Lodge, then yeah. That's what I was told."

"I'm Abigail Clark. I am the new owner of Sunset Lodge. My sister and I bought it a few months ago. We were going to run it together, but she ended up staying in New York City for the time being."

Abigail started to hold out a hand and then realized that she was covered in paint. She tried to cover the aborted gesture by reaching up to tuck a stray strand of hair behind her ear. The hair tie that she'd used to pull back her shoulder-length bob this morning wasn't doing a great job keeping her hair in place. Not that it mattered, as her light brown hair was undoubtedly covered in off-white paint now.

"I'm Barry," the man replied.

"Barry?" Abigail echoed.

"Barry Cuda."

"Oh, the boat guy," Abigail said as she finally remembered what she'd been told. "Someone told me that you used to manage the boat rentals for the Xanzibar Hotel."

Barry nodded. "That was a long time ago, though. The Xanzibar's been shut for decades."

"I was told you worked for Scott Wright for a while, too," Abigail said, trying to remember who had told her about Barry.

"I did," Barry replied flatly, a scowl momentarily flashing across the man's face.

Abigail hesitated. "The thing is, I'm doing everything I can to get the lodge back up and running. Jack and Janet Johnstone, the previous owners, stopped doing boat rentals years ago, but as we're right on Foxglove Lake, I'd love to be able to start offering them again."

"Could work. No one else is doing boat rentals right now. Scott Wright used to do them, but he stopped a few years back because he wasn't making enough money off of them. Some things aren't about money, though. Kids around here used to get to grow up on the lake. There were rowboats and canoes and pedal boats, all for rent. Kids could fish or just row out into the lake and have a picnic. Problem is insurance is expensive, at least according to Scott Wright."

Abigail frowned. "I hadn't thought of that. I'll have to make a few phone calls, I guess. I don't have a lot of extra money in the budget for insurance." Or anything else at this point, she added silently.

"So why were you looking for me?"

"It was suggested that you might be interested in running the boat rentals for me."

Barry shrugged and then scratched his head. "Maybe. I'm semi-retired now, but it might be fun to spend some time on the lake, renting out boats and fishing in between customers."

"Of course, the first thing we need to do is figure out if we actually have any boats or not."

"You don't know? What did Jack and Janet tell you?"

"That they'd locked up several canoes and pedal boats in the boathouse at the end of the summer season about ten years ago and then simply never bothered to open the boathouse again."

Barry frowned. "Someone could have stolen everything they had. If it's all still there, it could be in terrible condition."

"Mandy, that's my sister, and I walked down to the boathouse when we took our first tour of the property, but it was padlocked shut. Jack couldn't find the key for the padlock, so we never got to look inside."

"What made you and sister decide to buy Sunset Lodge, then? You said she's in New York City?"

"She is," Abigail agreed. "We were both there until a few months ago. I was managing a small boutique hotel with a gourmet restaurant attached and she was working two jobs she hated while hoping to land her dream job. We'd always talked about buying a business together one day and when Mandy saw a listing for Sunset Lodge somewhere, she suggested that we seriously consider buying it."

"But then she stayed behind?"

"Just before we were due to move here, she was offered her dream job. She studied technical theater in college and she was offered a chance to design sets for a production that is only just off-Broadway. It could lead to bigger and better things or it could be her one chance to do what she's always wanted to do before she comes here and helps run Sunset Lodge for the rest of her life."

"And that leaves you on your own to run it for now."

"Yeah, and it's a big job, but I have a lot of help, too."

"Is Marcia still in the kitchen?"

Abigail nodded. "I kept everyone who was working here when we bought the lodge." Marcia Burton had been cooking breakfast and dinner for lodge guests for over twenty years.

"You kept Catastrophe Carl?"

"'Catastrophe Carl?'"

Barry laughed. "Carl Young was the lodge's general handyman for years and years. He probably started working here before you were even born. He got the nickname when he tried his hand at some electrical work and nearly blew up the entire town. He's a decent handyman, though, as long as you don't need him to do anything electrical."

"He's still here."

"I'm surprised he isn't on the ladder, doing the painting for you."

"He's been painting the guest rooms," she explained. "And having extra days off as well. I'm trying to give everyone time off while we don't have any guests."

"It's October. I can't imagine you'll have any guests between now and May."

"Actually, we have several guests arriving toward the end of the month," Abigail replied, trying not to sound smug. "We advertised a special Halloween weekend getaway and filled all of the rooms that we currently have available."

"A Halloween getaway? What does that involve?"

"Mandy is working out the details, but basically we're going to decorate the lodge and having pumpkin carving and apple bobbing and that sort of thing. Marcia is putting together a special menu for the weekend and I'm trying to find someone to tell ghost stories around the fire and take people on hay rides."

"I may be able to help you there."

"With the ghost stories or the hay rides?"

"Both, although I was thinking more of the ghost stories. I belong to the Nightshade Players. We're a group of actors who get together occasionally to put on a play or maybe a musical if we're feeling especially ambitious. It's been a few years since we did much of anything, but years ago we used to put together a haunted house every October. I'm sure some of us still have costumes that mostly fit. We could take turns coming up and wandering around the lodge, scaring people, if you want, otherwise, we could just come and tell ghost stories and add atmosphere to the place."

"I don't think I want you to scare anyone, but a few ghouls or ghosts wandering around would definitely add atmosphere. I'm not sure I have the budget for that, though."

Barry shrugged. "I can't speak for everyone, but I'd be happy to come up for a few hours one day just for the fun of it. It's been a long time since I've had an excuse to dress up, not that I need one."

"Can you talk to the rest of the group about it, or should I call someone?"

"I can talk to everyone. I'll call Neal later and let him organize it. He loves to be in charge."

"Have him call me, then," she suggested. She was only a few steps away from the reception desk. There, she grabbed one of her business cards and held it out to the man. "He can call me anytime."

Barry glanced at the card and then slipped it into his pocket. "Does Arnold still work here?"

"Arnold Nagel? He's our night manager."

"His wife, Karen, did a show with us once. We tried to talk Arnold into being in it, too, because there was a perfect part for a man who pumps iron all day, but he wasn't interested. He said he couldn't make it to rehearsals because of his hours here."

"He works behind the desk late every night and early every morning and he's on call in between those sessions," Abigail replied. "I can't imagine when he'd have time to rehearse for a play."

Barry shrugged. "Joe took the part. He looks like a bodybuilder in his own mind, at least."

Abigail laughed. "I'm starting to look forward to meeting the rest of the Nightshade Players."

"I'm sure they'll be happy to do something. As I said, it's been a while."

"I can't pay much," Abigail warned him.

"We never got paid in the past. Any money we made from ticket sales always went back into the group to pay for costumes and props and sets for the next show." He paused and then laughed. "We used to have a party on the last night of show, too. That was always paid for out of ticket sales, too, which usually meant that we ended up with only a few dollars left for whatever we needed for the next show."

"If I don't have to pay you, I'd be more than happy to feed you all when you're here. As I said, Marcia is going to be putting together a special menu for the weekend. She can easily cook for a few extra people."

"I won't say no to that," Barry replied. "I love Marcia's cooking and I don't get to have it very often. She always brings the best dishes to the Christmas Festival."

"Christmas Festival?"

"You haven't heard about the Nightshade Christmas Festival yet?"

Abigail shook her head.

"It's an annual tradition, started years and years ago. Actually, I think it was probably started by Herb and Tammy Fuhrman back during the month or two that they owned the Xanzibar. It was called the Nightshade Hotel in those days, and they started the Nightshade Christmas Festival to help attract guests to the hotel in December."

"And the festival continued even after they sold the hotel?"

"The festival didn't even start until after they sold the hotel," he laughed. "As I said earlier, they only owned the hotel for a month or two. It opened in June or July and they'd sold it by the end of August, I think. I was managing the boat rentals for them, but they didn't say anything to anyone about the sale, not before or after. The first we knew about it was when we got our paychecks from somewhere else."

"Wow."

"We didn't know what to make of it, but we'd all been given a small raise, so none of us complained," he remembered.

"And then you had the first Christmas Festival?"

"Oh, yeah, that's what we were talking about. Yeah, Tammy had been planning this big Christmas Festival and even after the hotel was sold, she kept on planning. The event has changed a lot since then, of course, but it's still a big thing for Nightshade."

"What happens at the Christmas Festival now, then?"

"Well, for a start, it's now called the Nightshade Winter Festival," Barry replied with a scowl. "Scott Wright is the main sponsor now and he insisted that we change the name to be more inclusive, whatever that means. They set up a dozen huge tents across the baseball and soccer fields at the town park. Scott pays to have big heaters put in every tent, which is why he gets to name the event. I suppose I should be grateful he hasn't renamed it the Wright Festival or something like that."

Abigail grinned. "And what happens in all of the tents?"

"One will be full of people selling crafty stuff. Another is more like a yard sale. It takes place the week before Christmas, so both tents are really popular. There's one tent full of cookies and other baked goods. Another has carnival-type games, including everyone's favorite dunk tank. The high school principal and a few other notable folks from around town each take a turn at the dunk tank."

"It all sounds like fun."

"For a small town like Nightshade, it's a big deal. If you like that sort of thing, though, you should drive over to Ramsey. They have events like that every single month."

"Really? I may have to check some of them out. Is this the only event that happens in Nightshade?"

"Nah, there's a fair in the summer and an apple festival in the fall, too. The Christmas Festival is the best, though."

Abigail nodded. "I wonder if people outside of Nightshade would be interested in our Christmas, er, Winter Festival. I'm going to have to find out more about it."

"Talk to Scott Wright. He's in charge. If he likes you, he'll probably let you make lots of changes to it as well."

"I don't want to change anything. I just want to figure out the best way to promote the event to potential guests."

Barry's eyes narrowed slightly. "I reckon you and Scott will get along just fine," he muttered.

Feeling as if she'd angered the man, Abigail changed the subject. "But we were talking about boats," she said. "I assume the lake freezes over in the winter months?"

"Yeah, lots of people go out ice fishing and Scott sets up an ice rink near the center of town."

"So we won't be able to start renting out boats until spring."

He nodded. "And you probably won't find many people interested in going out on the lake until late spring. It can still feel quite cold on the lake in April."

"So if we were going to advertise boating, it would be for the summer months," Abigail said, mostly talking to herself.

"June, July, and August," Barry agreed. "Maybe September, but it rains a lot in September. The kind of folks who rent rowboats or pedal boats to splash around Foxglove Lake for an hour or two aren't going to bother in the rain."

Abigail nodded. "I'm not sure it will be worth the time and effort to reopen the boathouse."

"We should probably start by seeing what's down there. If you wanted to open this summer, you may need to start ordering parts or even replacement boats."

"Yes, that's a good point. Do you have time now to take a look?"

Barry shrugged. "I don't have anything else to do."

Wishing she could say the same, Abigail picked up her paint can. "Give me a minute to clean up and we'll go and see what we find."

There was a utility sink in the large room next to the kitchen that also housed two industrial-sized washing machines and dryers. Abigail rinsed her brush and then wrapped it in plastic wrap. "I'll be back for you soon," she told the brush as she put it on a nearby shelf. After replacing the lid on the paint can, she spent several minutes scrubbing her hands and lower arms, trying to remove as much as possible. A quick look in the mirror by the door showed her that her face and hair were both covered in splatters and spots of beige paint.

"It doesn't matter," she muttered as she walked back toward the lobby.

"What doesn't matter?" Marcia asked from inside the kitchen.

Abigail laughed. "I'm a mess. I wouldn't normally go outside looking like this, but Barry is here, so we're going to walk down to the boathouse and see what Jack and Janet left behind."

Marcia made a face. "I can't imagine you'll find much that's still seaworthy. That boathouse has been locked up tight for ten years or more."

"Maybe Barry can use all of the parts from what's down there to make at least one or two useable boats. It would be a start, at least."

"Good luck," Marcia told her.

Barry was sitting in front of the fireplace, his legs stretched out in front of him when Abigail reached the lobby. His eyes were closed and as she approached him, she realized that he was snoring quietly. As she tried to work out the best way to wake him, she thought about keys. Jack and Janet had told her that they hadn't been able to find the key to the padlock on the boathouse door, but it was still probably worth taking the ring of keys that they had given her. They may have been mistaken.

She went into the office and pulled out the large ring of keys. It was helpfully labeled "Miscellaneous Keys." Slamming the desk drawer shut, she clomped loudly back into the lobby.

Barry opened one eye. "I hear yah," he muttered.

Abigail crossed to the door as he slowly got to his feet.

"I'm not sure why the boathouse is so far away," she said as they began to follow the path from the lodge toward the lake.

"I was told that Jack's dad, when he had the boathouse built, didn't want to block the views of the lake from the main building," Barry told her. "He thought the boathouse was unsightly."

The path led directly to the lake. A second path ran along the edge of the lake before disappearing into a cluster of trees, shrubs, and long grass.

"You're going to need to have someone clear this path," Barry remarked as Abigail tried to stomp down the tall grass.

"It's further than I remembered," she muttered as the path went around a curve and then headed back toward the lake. "And uglier," she added when the boathouse came into view.

Barry laughed. "It's just a shack, really, but it wouldn't take much effort to improve it. You could paint it, for a start. It looks as if it needs a new roof, too."

Abigail sighed. "We should have taken a closer look at this before we bought the lodge. I can't afford to put a new roof on this place, not right away."

"I can probably patch what's up there. Don't give up yet," Barry told her. "Let's see how bad it is inside, first."

Long grass and thick sand made the last part of the walk to the door difficult. There two steps led up to a battered wooden porch. Abigail looked at the padlock and then at her keys.

"I don't think any of these are the right size for this lock," she said. Two minutes later, she'd checked every key. None of them fit. "We're going to need bolt cutters or something," she said with a sigh.

Barry shook his head. "It's a cheap padlock. I can pick it."

"Pick it?" Abigail echoed.

He looked at the lock and then back at her. "It doesn't look all that old, really. This hasn't been here for ten years.

She was surprised when Barry pulled a small pouch out of his pocket. He pulled a few thin tools out of the pouch and then went to work on the lock. Less than a minute later, he grinned at her.

"Easy as pie," he said as the lock opened. He removed it from the door and then slid back the bar that was holding the door shut.

"There isn't any power down here. We should have brought a flashlight," Abigail said as Barry pulled the door open.

He chuckled and then returned his lock picks to their case and put them in his pocket. When he pulled his hand out again, he was holding a small flashlight.

"It's pretty bright, especially for its size," he said as he switched it on.

"It smells terrible in there," Abigail said as she took a step forward.

"There are probably animals living in there."

Abigail shuddered as Barry shined the flashlight into one corner of the space.

"That's a rowboat," he said, slowly moving the light from left to right. "And another one. And a pedal boat, or what's left of one. And that's a skeleton."

Abigail swallowed hard as the light came to rest on the skeleton that appeared to be lying in one of the rowboats.

Alibis in Alpha Sector

Now available to pre-order – the first book in Diana's latest new series:

Alibis in Alpha Sector
A Lady Elizabeth Cozy in Space

Release date: September 14, 2022.

When I lost my low paying, dead-end job, a friend offered me a one-way ticket to Val Segas. I didn't want to take advantage of his generosity, but we both knew that that ticket was probably the only way I'd ever get off Cenclare.

He surprised me with a ticket on the Lady Elizabeth, InmonCorp's newest luxury spacecraft. Even the cheapest, smallest cabins were supposed to be loaded with luxuries. When my elevator made an unscheduled stop on an unfinished deck before I'd even made it to my cabin, things got complicated fast.

After finding a dying man in what was meant to be an empty corridor, I found myself being bribed with a long list of upgrades, clearly designed to get me to keep quiet about what I'd seen. The bribes might have worked, too, if it wasn't for the man I'd been sharing the elevator with when it made its unscheduled stop.

Colonel Jonathan Brazee is determined to conduct his own investigation into what he is convinced was murder, and he seems equally insistent on dragging me along for the ride. All I know is that I'll be a lot happier if I don't have to spend the next twenty-six sectors traveling with a killer.

Also by Diana Xarissa

The Isle of Man Cozy Mysteries

Aunt Bessie Provides

Aunt Bessie Questions

Aunt Bessie Remembers

Aunt Bessie Solves

Aunt Bessie Tries

Aunt Bessie Understands

Aunt Bessie Volunteers

Aunt Bessie Wonders

Aunt Bessie's X-Ray

Aunt Bessie Yearns

Aunt Bessie Zeroes In

The Aunt Bessie Cold Case Mysteries

The Adams File

The Bernhard File

The Carter File

The Durand File

The Evans File

The Flowers File

The Goodman File

The Howard File

The Markham Sisters Cozy Mystery Novellas

The Appleton Case

The Bennett Case

The Chalmers Case

The Donaldson Case

The Janet Markham Bennett Cozy Thrillers

The Doyle Assignment

The Everest Assignment

The Farnsley Assignment

The George Assignment

The Hamilton Assignment

The Isle of Man Romances

Island Escape

Island Inheritance

Island Heritage

Island Christmas

The Later in Life Love Stories

Second Chances

Second Act

Second Thoughts

Second Degree

Second Best

Second Nature

Second Place

Bookplates Are Now Available

Would you like a signed bookplate for this book?

I now have bookplates (stickers) that I can personalize, sign, and send to you. It's the next best thing to getting a signed copy!

Send an email to diana@dianaxarissa.com with your mailing address (I promise not to use it for anything else, ever) and how you'd like your bookplate personalized and I'll sign one and send it to you.

There is no charge for a bookplate, but there is a limit of one per person.

About the Author

Diana has been self-publishing since 2013, and she feels surprised and delighted to have found readers who enjoy the stories and characters that she imagines. Always an avid reader, she still loves nothing more than getting lost in fictional worlds, her own or others!

After being raised in Erie, Pennsylvania, and studying history at Allegheny College in Meadville, Pennsylvania, Diana pursued a career in college administration. She was living and working in Washington, DC, when she met her future husband, an Englishman who was visiting the city.

Following her marriage, Diana moved to Derbyshire. A short while later, she and her husband relocated to the Isle of Man. After ten years on the island, during which Diana earned a Master's degree in the island's history, they made the decision to relocate again, this time to the US.

Now living near Buffalo, New York, Diana and her husband live with their daughter, a student at the University at Buffalo. Their son is now living and working just outside of Boston, Massachusetts, giving Diana an excuse to travel now and again.

Diana also writes mystery/thrillers set in the not-too-distant future as Diana X. Dunn and Young Adult fiction as D.X. Dunn.

She is always happy to hear from readers. You can write to her at:

Diana Xarissa Dunn
PO Box 72
Clarence, NY 14031.

Find Diana at: DianaXarissa.com
E-mail: Diana@dianaxarissa.com

Printed in Great Britain
by Amazon

83736323R00119